THE MESSAGE
FROM THE HORSE

···

THE MESSAGE FROM THE HORSE

Klaus Ferdinand Hempfling

Translated by David Walser

TRAFALGAR SQUARE
North Pomfret, Vermont

First published in the English language in 2015 by
Trafalgar Square Books
North Pomfret, Vermont 05053

Originally published in the German language as *Die Botschaft der Pferde* by
Franckh-Kosmos Verlags-GmbH & Co., Stuttgart

Trafalgar Square Books encourages the use of approved safety helmets in all
equestrian sports.

ISBN: 978-1-57076-748-7
Library of Congress Control Number: 2015948722

Book design by Lauryl Eddlemon
Cover design by RM Didier
Cover photos courtesy of Klaus Ferdinand Hempfling
Typeface: Electra
Printed in Canada

10 9 8 7 6 5 4 3 2 1

*It is not the truth that a person feels he
possesses but the quality of the effort he
has made to get behind the truth.
That is what measures a man's worth.*

–Gotthold Ephraim Lessing

CONTENTS

....

Preface   *ix*

Part I

The Silent Ones' Message   *1*

Part II

The Soft Breeze Wafted Over the Lake   *19*

Part III

The Sun Follows Its Course and the
    Scents of Nature Respond to Its Passage   *45*

Part IV

He Is Not There to Carry Man's Grief   *95*

Part V

They Called It "The Other World"   *131*

preface

THE SULTRY AIR HUNG above us like a sponge about to be squeezed. The animals and the rest of us waited, as if we all shared the same thought: when might a deafening thunderclap bring it to an end? My breath was short and fast; a cold sweat ran down my spine.

The old monk sat facing me in his armchair, his gaze fixed on the infinite. Barely perceptibly, his lips began to move.

"You have come to learn from me. That is good. But you are expecting explanations. That is *not* good. How does it help to smother everything in words? Of course, people feel at home when you do so: it is the disease of our times.

"What you and others are looking for cannot be reached by words alone. It is alien and new, as unique as every individual is in this world.

"To reach a true understanding with the tools we are given is almost impossible. We have to venture into the unknown and this requires courage, strength, and an open, watchful spirit. Fear of the boundaries of this new land is the chief enemy. The truth you seek recognizes no frontiers. You must be willing to go in any direction."

The old man's breathing was as regular and calm as his speech.

His gaze appeared to be concentrated on something invisible to my eyes. After a long pause he continued.

"And how do you recognize the truth? Truth is life itself. That is why it is powerful and dangerous: where the day is, there can be no night. Truth leads you back to yourself and to all that is natural. It cures your dependency and drives away the dark fruit of your fears.

"How do you set out on this quest for the truth? You must first abandon the little room that gives you your feeling of security but imprisons you. You will begin to understand the truth when you seek it with all your senses, with your entire being…"

He turned his level gaze on me as he went on, "My words alone can never explain it all to you. They can only scratch the surface of all the wisdom spoken by the sages of old. Their true worth stays hidden."

"And where is it hidden? Where can I find it?" I asked impatiently.

"Where can you find it?" he murmured as his gaze once again focused on something infinitely distant. Then, almost in a whisper, he continued, "Everything, however far apart, is connected."

"And how does this answer what I am looking for?"

"You asked me where you would find the truth. You are finding it this very instant. You will find it in what people flippantly call 'nothingness.'"

After a while I rose to my feet and left. The monk sat silent and motionless.

PART I

....

The Silent Ones' Message

one

IT IS EARLY EVENING and thoughts are forming in my mind without leading in any particular direction. It is not so that in this world all our thoughts are somehow part of a planned design and lead to an expected conclusion. No, they often come on silent footsteps, leading us in directions we had not planned or foreseen. They come as quietly as my horse's gentle breathing and sometimes last no longer than a single breath.

My horse is white, with a black mane. He is still a young stallion, but I see time creeping up on him as his mane pales a little more each year. As I feel him beneath me and think about him, life and death no longer hold any terrors. I am part of this horse and we experience life together: not life as perhaps I *should* see it but, dare I say it, life as it really is.

I live in this magic environment: the fire-red stones, the precipitous cliffs, the desiccated vegetation, the tortuous channels gouged out by winter streams that for a short time spring into life; the golden sands that light up and glitter with the low autumnal sun lying on the horizon; the iron-rich rocks that seem to have split or exploded and demonstrate a degree of hidden strength that one cannot ignore—indeed, a force that I take in with every breath.

This is where I live, in the valley of the ravens. On the horizon, gigantic rock formations reach into the sky as if being drawn upward to share in the might of the heavens. The landscape is peppered with ancient ruins, half-collapsed walls of old forts and dwellings, all woven together by the magicians of past centuries—fragmentary quotations that describe the passing of time but still radiate strength, life, and beauty.

I feel blessed to live here in this land called Catalonia, which reaches from the Spanish foothills of the Pyrenees, up over the precipitous mountains and down into the French plains.

On evenings like this I while away the hours in my horse's company on the little terrace in front of the old house, breathing in the unparalleled beauty of this corner of the world. I know my horse also feels the energy these moments give us, and the resulting calm that settles on us. I allow my gaze to wander, taking in every new detail of a landscape that is picking itself up after the energy-crushing dryness and heat of the endless summer months. Here and there, flashes of green announce the imminent arrival of the wet period, the fleeting springtime before the crushing heat of the sun returns for another year.

And this is how it is in winter: the sun is mild and gentle and a friend to man and beast. The nights are chilly and draw us all to the fires that burn continuously. When the ice-cold air that gathers in the valley beneath climbs toward us, the animals gather by the walls of the house and press themselves close against the warm stones.

"Come quickly! You must come now! The little stallion—they've driven him into the steel cage—he's bleeding all over and now he can't get out. You must come quickly!"

Fernando, our neighbor's chubby son, has climbed the steep hill below us as fast as he can manage and only just has enough wind to shout out his message toward the rear wall of the house. He can't see me but must have guessed that at this time of day I would be working with one of my stallions behind the half tumbled-down wall.

Finally his little round, red face appears in a large hole in the wall, and he repeats his message before I can say anything to calm him.

I have never seen this boy so animated before and decide to forego any questions: it is clearly an emergency. I lead my horse into his stall while I shout to Fernando to go straight to the jeep.

A minute later we are bouncing down the precipitous stony track; the sun is already low on the horizon and even though here in the mountains we are over 100 kilometers from the sea I have, as I often do on evenings like this, the sensation of being able to smell fish in the air. As soon as the sun sets, the smell disappears and is replaced by the strong odor of the pine trees that clothe the slopes.

In front of us, the old house looks across a wide dusty plateau; to the left of us the road, shored up by the ubiquitous, half-crumbled walls that cover the landscape, plunges down to the valley.

Fernando points in an agitated manner with his little arms toward a group of men in front of us. "There they are, the idiots, and now they don't know what to do!"

"Calm down, Fernando! Let's first see what's happened."

We pull up in front of the group, which stands aside. The boy leaps out and starts to run toward the cage before Antonio stops him.

"You stay put, Fernando, do you hear?"

Only now can I see the tragedy: they've driven Pinto, a fiery young stallion, into the narrow steel cage, which is big enough to contain a bullock or a small horse but without leaving the creature the smallest room for movement. Whole herds are trapped by using this dreadful contraption. When the front and back gates of the cage are closed, no resistance is possible. In this case the stallion is thrashing about in such a panic that in addition they have used a *serreta*, a veritable instrument of torture. Sharp spikes are digging into the tenderest part of the horse's nostrils and the rope attached to the *serreta* is now tangled around one of his forelegs. Any attempt to move him or indeed free him from the cage only increases his panic and tears his nostrils even more severely.

Antonio, the manager, comes toward me, saying, "*Este caballo es malo, malo, malo!*" "He's a bad, bad, bad horse!"

Through gritted teeth, I take a deep breath before greeting him as civilly as I can.

"You've a problem here," I say. "What happened?"

He replies but I am not really listening. I slowly approach the cage. I see the *serreta*, which by now has reduced the nostrils to a bleeding lump of flesh, and my blood boils. I pause a moment as Antonio looks questioningly at me. I go toward Jose.

"Give me your knife," I say, "and now beat on the back of the cage with your stick!" He looks over momentarily at his father, but Antonio is impassive and nods without saying a word. The youth does what I ask, and the little stallion jerks his head upward in fright and to one side. Now I can get hold of the rope to sever it. At this point his front foreleg is so bent that he is almost lying on his side; the right hind leg has slipped through the bars of the cage and every convulsion only aggravates his situation. I ask the group of men to back away from the cage and give me space.

I gaze into the evening sky at the setting sun. I feel the calm. I feel the tension draining away. I feel the chaos of the situation like a knot—one that can gradually be undone. And so I finally calm the stallion.

"Be still, little horse! Be still!" I know I have to get close to him without causing another panic attack. "Hand me a rope, please, Jose!"

I can see that Antonio and the others trust me enough to leave me alone. Suddenly I feel as if I am observing the scene from a distance. I am aware of a change of scents in the air: The wind has veered to the southwest, and it is pleasantly warm as it blows softly up from the valley below, carrying the heavy scent of the herbs that carpet the hillside. I breathe deeply and slowly, relishing the beautiful, mild evening; I feel the warmth of the sun on my left cheek and the breeze ruffling my hair. Once again I take a deep breath and enjoy the soft, balmy air. My fingertips begin to stroke the sweat-drenched neck of the little stallion. His eyes are now half closed and he has become completely calm. Only the horse can hear my voice as I describe the beauty of the evening to him.

For a moment or two I consider whether to remove the painful *serreta* but decide against it. My first task is to get him out of the steel cage. Only then can I decide what course to take.

I start by feeding the rope under the angled foreleg and then around his neck. In doing so, I make it clear to him that, with one big heave, he must stand up. I pass the end of the rope over the top bar of the cage and give it to Antonio, asking him and the three others to pull on it with all their strength when I give the order. I walk quietly around to the other side of the cage and carefully pass another rope around the ankle joint of the trapped hind leg. I gaze out over the sweat-covered body of the horse and across the valley to the dark red sunset. My hand rests on the horse's croup and I feel the little fellow breathing calmly. He gives a tentative snort through the blood that clogs his nostrils.

It has only been a few minutes since we met, but already the mysterious bond between us is in place. The nature of this bond cannot be properly put into words. It is an indescribable sensation that rises from one's innermost being, a pulsing, a soaring instant of awareness, a flash of understanding that one might doubt had taken place if it were not for the fact that the horse lies there peacefully, waiting and trusting.

"*Tira! Tira! Tira!*" "Pull! Pull! Pull!" I shout toward the men and in the same instant I pull with all my strength on the rope that will free the trapped hind leg. With a terrific crack the horse strikes his head on the metal bars; he rears up with his left foreleg hanging outside the cage. Again he strikes the cage bars with a loud crack of his head. "Come on, boy! Once more, one more effort!" are the words going through my mind.

I say to the men, "When he rears up again, pull like demons!" At the same time I increase the pull on my rope, as I shout, "NOW!"

Again the horse strikes his head a fearful blow on the cage bars and then I am falling backward until I am stopped by hitting my own head on a post. I can still hear the sound of his hooves striking the steel bars, and I right myself in time to see him galloping away.

Meanwhile Antonio has walked over to me and is asking if all is well.

"Thank you! Thank you!" I say. "I'm okay."

"*Este caballo es malo, malo, malo,*" says Antonio, shaking his head.

"No!" I say under my breath. "It's you, not he, who is bad."

two

I BELIEVE I AM INDEBTED first and foremost to the horses themselves for my understanding of how to deal with situations that require instantaneous action. It is they who have taught me to find inner peace, to live completely in the moment, to marry my existence to theirs and be part of the great current that embraces all living creatures in a state of total trust; to be one who watches with all my senses and concentration, recognizing that the distinction between good and bad luck has no relevance: it is only life that matters, life as opposed to not-life.

The stallion is now standing quietly enough in a corner of the fenced area. The *serreta* is still clamped deep into his nostrils and clearly causes him dreadful pain every time he breathes, and even more so when he lowers his head and treads by mistake on the short piece of rope attached to it.

Antonio comes over to me and goes on about what an awful horse this is, the worst he has ever experienced, that won't allow anyone near him and only reacts with biting and kicking. This, he explains, is the reason for using the steel cage.

I have already worked with a lot of horses that were more dangerous than this one. What makes the situation special is the injury this stallion has suffered. The pain and the panic, and not his true nature, now dictate his reactions. Before I can do anything I have to reduce the pain.

Jose, Fernando, and the rest are standing on the other side of the fence and volunteering unhelpful remarks. I hear Antonio repeating his warning to me to mind myself because this is such a bad horse, and I wonder how such a basically good man could get things so wrong.

By now dusk has fallen. It is a clear evening but the bright moon has not yet driven off the red sunset, which gives our scene an unreal quality.

Jose brings me a long rope; I carefully drive the young stallion into a corner of the fencing. In spite of all his pain he seems to understand that I have his interests at heart. I now have to do something totally different from what I would usually do. I move closer and closer toward his croup and by means of little signals I get him to understand that he should turn his head toward me. With barely perceptible movements I am trying to build a common space in which he will accept me as a trusted horse—and one senior to himself.

A situation like this follows the same path: it is a game in which the two sides learn about each other at a certain distance. The ceremony lasts only a few minutes, but out of it springs a deep and friendly relationship in which the rank of the participants is made absolutely clear. The horse can then face me with trust and without fear. He accepts me and knows that he is accepted for what he is.

But there is still a very thorny problem I have to face: I've prepared a large loop with the rope in my hands and at some point I have to throw it around his neck. The little stallion turns his head toward me, and I lift my left hand high enough to throw the noose over his head with a single motion — but at that precise moment I see that I have moved too fast.

Time freezes. I know the probable outcome, but there is nothing I can do except let my body react as it would naturally. Only in this way can I avoid disaster, but even as the event unfolds, I am considering how else I could have gone about it.

The stallion rears up and bends his head backward and in the last fraction of a second I have to take my arm as far back as I can in order to slip the rope over his head. I know I should have found another way to do this as with my last ounce of energy I swing my hips to one side — but not far enough: The stallion lands a hard kick to the right side of my pelvis. An intense pain shoots through my body. I see the shadows of the men watching as they move toward me and shout to them to keep away. With all the strength I can muster, I anchor my left leg to the ground; the rope goes taut and the stallion falls down.

He stares at me, and it is as if I am looking into his eyes for the first time: I see an intense and deep-seated look of sorrow.

I am drawn to anxious horses. Why is it I like them so much? Perhaps because I've pursued what you might call the sensitive, almost anxious, path in life, and for this reason I like sensitive and fragile horses. I have gone down the same road. Isn't it the timorous ones who must finally dare to overcome that timidity? Isn't it the sensitive ones who in the end set aside their fears? Hasn't it always been the hard-pressed, the failures, and the harassed that have risen in revolt?

three

IT IS NOT ONLY THIS that we have in common, but also the pain. I try to relax, breathing deeply. Very little of the men's state of excitement reaches me. I can't understand why it never occurs to me in situations like this to turn away and not become involved, but I know better than to resist the great current of life that sweeps us along.

Events now take their natural course. The horse has all his attention concentrated on me. We are both suppressing our pain in an effort to come out of this situation in which fate has involved us. Slowly, as if following a well-worn ritual, I begin to move my upper body. My right hand, holding the rope, has the measure of the problem, but I have to be totally concentrated because everything must work the first time. My leg hurts too much for me to be able to follow the horse or get out of his way.

"*Tranquilo, por favor,*" I call out to the men, in case any of them has not understood that I am no longer in danger. My relationship with the horse is sealed; the moment has arrived when I can ask him to come to me, to follow me, and indeed to trust me without hesitation.

I put all my weight onto my left leg and brace myself with the rope in my right hand; the stallion throws up his head and looks at me. I take a slow step backward, end our eye contact, and invite him in his own language to come toward me and to follow me. He makes a little enquiring snort and comes quietly over toward me. As if drawn by an invisible force, he comes to my hand with his head held low and follows my shaky footsteps.

Pain is still disrupting my concentration, but in the few minutes that are left to me I have to make it crystal clear to him that I am superior to him in rank. He moves toward me and places his lowered head against my chest so that I can try to open the *serreta*. As I put my hand on it, he jerks his head to one side but without the slightest sign of aggression, and takes a step backward, and then comes up close again. This time I am able to remove the blood-encrusted steel from his nose and place a halter that Jose has handed me around his neck.

None of the men utter a word; some of them make as if to come toward me, but Antonio holds them back. I know how ashamed he is of what has taken place as he quietly leads the stallion into his stall. I glance across at him and take my leave of the men. They ask me if they can help me in any way but I refuse, saying things are not really too bad. I maneuver my right leg gingerly across the driver's seat of my jeep and start the engine. Antonio catches my eye and calls out, "He's really docile. Extraordinary!"

"I'll be over in a day or two. Goodbye for now!" I call to him, but he's already walking over to me. I lower the window and he sticks his round, red, bullet-shaped head through the opening.

"*Gracias!*"

"*De nada — hombre!*" I reply and attempt a smile.

I drive up the dusty road until I reach the fork and continue a little way to the left before stopping. I move my leg tentatively before sitting quietly and breathing in the mild air of evening. I look to the left and let my eyes follow a stone wall that leads away into the twilight and the unending distance. The confusion of what has just happened begins to sink into my consciousness. It has been ages since I have been wounded by a horse and I have not yet come to terms with the reasons behind it.

four

A PAINFUL NIGHT FOLLOWS, and I am not much help to Emilio mucking out the stables the next morning. The pain in my hip is still severe and the swelling reaches right down to my knee.

It is a beautiful, sunny spring day. I throw a few things into the jeep because I have to drive down to where the land is flat and by day smells of fish, where the sea touches the city of nearly five million inhabitants.

My road takes me through a small village; on one side, a long row of dilapidated houses leans against the mountain and is bathed from morning till night in the rays of the low winter sun. As if I am the only living being moving across a painting, I drive past an old man in a blue jacket and dark cap, propped up against a wall.

Now the roads are a little wider as I approach the town. How I dislike towns, and yet in this part of the world there is always something that appeals to me: Even in the coldest part of the year, people seem unaware of the stinking buses and the noisy vehicles. Children play games; old men sit about on benches or in groups. Narrow as the streets become, there seems to be a place for this kind of activity that has all but disappeared from the cities of my homeland.

It has been some time since I have come here. In spite of the pain, I hobble along the wide pavement between lanes of traffic, under the plane trees, engrossed in my thoughts, past innumerable cafes and bars, little restaurants, and as many pigeons as people. I seek refuge from the midday heat in the shade of a café. At the next table a beggar is asking two girls for a cigarette. With friendly smiles, they give him a whole half pack. His eyes light up and I notice that under his arm is a cardboard carton with a bottle of cheap wine. The girls talk to him until the waiter arrives and chases him away. I sit watching the hustle and bustle around me, and I am aware of a deep unease inside me. I think of my mountains and yesterday's little stallion. How much untapped and unspoiled energy does he still have? At least he is alive!

But these people around me, jostling and hurrying—what makes them tick? What vision drives them? What moves them? What aim in life inspires them? What shining ambitions do they have? What adventures stimulate them? In all this hectic hubbub, what concerns them? What rewards do they expect? And even when they appear to be calm, what lies underneath in the hidden layers of their lives?

A young man sits down near me on the rim of a stone basin containing a palm tree, in order to feed his puppy. My mind wanders back over the past year, considering the ebb and flow of nature that has been my constant companion; I can hardly grasp the strange fact that this glittering, agitated world exists only a short drive away from the one in which I have been buried, and seemingly has no idea that anything different exists. At this very moment I am aware of the contrast more than ever before. The hustle and bustle that surrounds me, the playful shadows of the bare plane trees, the rays of the setting sun on the rough walls of the café, all help to soften the constant, crippling pain in my hip and the memory of the desperate little stallion struggling to save himself. Unformed thoughts whirl about in my consciousness, but at the same time I am aware of the newfound strength and joy that the little chap must be experiencing.

I wonder if it would ever be possible to see and to hear the world through the eyes and ears of a horse. With his senses, how would my understanding of what I would call life, strength, or feelings be experienced? How would I think of being really stretched as opposed to being politely exercised? Would it ever be possible to describe what I experience when I allow the wonders of nature to touch me or indeed to penetrate my being down to the very doors of my soul?

Some people think of me as a charlatan; they believe that my relationship with horses is somehow dependent on hypnosis and magic tricks. But I ask you: Is not what I do a reflection of the most basic and simplest form of life, a life in which the brotherhood of every living creature is apparent?

I linger a while in this pleasant spot, which seems like an island of sanity in the turmoil of the city. Since I feel no urge to hurry on, I remain, engrossed in my thoughts a little longer. It is not really so important to record what I actually do as to try to share the almost indescribable secrets that lie behind what I do. This is what I need to do for my own peace of mind and for the sake of the horses—and, indeed, for other people.

Still deep in my thoughts, I climb back into the jeep; the pain that had calmed a little during the day now reasserts itself. I turn on the radio for distraction and listen to some twentieth-century music. For a few kilometers the lights of the city keep me company, but then I turn onto a small country road that leads up into my hills, back to my horses and the world I understand.

The jeep's old diesel motor bears me along at a leisurely pace as the road winds slowly upward. The moon shines bright and the trees cast long black shadows that settle my thoughts and give a peaceful rhythm to my progress. Driving is not my favorite occupation but on this occasion I enjoy the journey. The pain in my hip drapes like a thin veil over my being and is hardly noticeable. I let my thoughts lead me where they want to, combining the happenings of the day with the possibilities of the future. It seems as if the spirit revels in a peaceful warm space and wanders quietly in and out of reality to a dream world in which anything can happen. I am taken back to my early days in the mountains when this part of my life took root, and it presents me with difficult memories that are almost too powerful to relive: the first encounters with the wild horses and the time I shared with the old monk. Paloma makes a sudden appearance, high up in the semi-deserted village, and Puitschmal—the "evil mountain"—and that unforgettable, moonless night within the crumbling walls of the monastery. And then, of course, old Valenciano is there, too.

My thoughts lead me back along my life's path, a long and difficult journey, but one that has not finished yet and never will. A path that will take me to the limits of understanding and the gates of the great unknown.

For some time the road has become ever more steep and bumpy. Having to engage the four-wheel drive announces our imminent arrival. I park behind the house just as Emilio is closing the last stall doors.

"Another day over!" I say to him. He has drawn down his hat over his ears and his forehead, but his twinkling, well-disposed eyes stare at me out of his small, creased face. Standing by a half-open stall he hesitates a moment and then says, " Yes, another day less!"

"Yes," I reply, taking his point, "another day less."

five

I QUITE OFTEN WORK and play with my horses late into the night, but on this evening, I do a quick check to see that all is well and sit myself down next to the fire. I will have plenty of time in the next few days and I need to turn all the conflicting thoughts that fill my mind from the day's events into concrete plans for the future. Is there any possibility of putting into words what cannot easily, if at all, be written down? Is it not the path already walked in life that helps a person reach into the depths of the self and arrive at understanding? Would it not be possible for me to identify the key moments along this way that drove me relentlessly onward so that I could share them with other people? And could this lead on to that knowledge that governs my life today? And finally, would I be led to an understanding of that painful incident with the little stallion?

I ease myself a little closer to the fireplace, and as I begin to put down, not without some difficulty, the words of my saga, the cold air settles in the valley below me and the horses press up closely against the warm stones of the old walls.

PART II

....

The Soft Breeze Wafted
Over the Lake

one

YES, I STILL REMEMBER the time exactly. I had only been a few days up in the mountains, and it was as if a mysterious force drew me to a particular spot. These were days of waiting, of uncertainty, of farewells and new beginnings. I remember quite clearly that afternoon when I, as it were, buried myself in the cavity of a rock in order to escape the cold wind that was keening from the northeast. It was the time of year when the weather reinvented itself and all nature took refuge.

I had still not exchanged more than a couple of words with the old monk. Again and again he withdrew and seemed to avoid the issue with strange, brief explanations. It was only much later that I realized that even at this early stage he was carefully laying the foundations of a structure that would only reveal its true shape later on. In the meantime I felt rejected and unsure of where I stood in my struggle with the forces of nature.

And now the cold had set in: the mighty Puitschmal mountain — the "evil mountain," as it is known to the locals—reared up in front of me, and below, in stark contrast, lay the black expanse of the lake. I crouched even farther back in the rock cavity, waiting for the rain that always follows in these conditions. I raised my eyes to follow the flight of a heron as it sank slowly down toward the water, but then watched it lift up again toward the rock face with a few powerful strokes of its wings.

I witnessed what I had not expected at this time of the year. Soon it would be spring, but snow still lay up in the mountains so the heron still had time to explore different sites for its nest.

I watched a little mare quietly going about her business, the grayness of the lowering cloud being so close to the color of her coat that she disappeared and reappeared from view, minute by minute, in the most mysterious way. I could sense that her gait was labored as if she were tired, but though my gaze was concentrated on her, I felt no corresponding emotion.

At this point, I began to feel stronger, as though something in me was about to snap. My back was curved so that my insides felt uncomfortably compressed, but I raised my eyes and calmly connected with the passage of the horses. An intense trembling took hold of me as I filled my lungs with the cool, clear air. The stillness seemed almost unbearable: without thinking, I put my hands up to my mouth in the shape of a trumpet, took a deep breath, and feeling as if all my life wanted to break out of me, I shouted as loudly as I could to the evening sky.

"*Yegua, Yegua, Yegua!*" "Little mare!"

The echo of my shout returned, the words falling over each other, cleaving the wind and the stillness, but the mysterious comings and goings of the horses continued. Once again I raised my hands to form a loudspeaker and shouted defiance at the unimaginable power of what lay before my eyes: the mountain, the lake, the clouds, the horses, and yes, the little mare.

Just in front of me there was a large stone, so large that I could not lift it, but I dragged it to the edge of the abyss and pushed it over. Time slowed as I watched it fall, and I had the sensation that I perceived it as the one visible mark of my existence.

The momentum caused by pushing the stone dragged my body perilously forward until my foot found purchase on the stump of a tree. As if I had received a blow, my blood ran cold, and I watched the stone bounce off an overhang. It split into two: both parts struck the water at the same time. The water stirred, but soon the ripples ceased and the calm of a thousand years was restored.

Slowly my tears began to flow and it seemed as if a calm had penetrated the innermost parts of my soul. I was hardly aware of the damp and cold of the evening that was by now affecting me. However, I felt as if, somewhere inside me, a dam had been breached and a little light had reached hidden parts of my being. I felt a life force combining with the sense of calm.

My gaze lit on the house below me in the valley, and I could see that the old monk had started a fire. The scent of burning lavender wood filled my nostrils, and through the small window panes I could see the bright red light of the flickering flames, contrasting with the dark green, blue, and black outside.

By that time it was getting colder. The horses had vanished; the soft wind was wafting across the lake; heaven and earth had agreed to combine forces and bury their differences. These opposing powers understood they had to live in harmony.

I rose stiffly to my feet. I knew it would not rain again that day as I watched the moonlight flickering across the fissured wall of the nearest mountain. Nature, as if suffering from exhaustion, was resting quietly, and the wind was casting its spell on the shimmering water. I thought of the horses and their secret, which I had set myself the task of discovering. The fire down below drew me toward its comforting warmth and showed me my way through the darkness.

two

THE OLD MONK SAT facing me. This was our first proper meeting at which no one said a word. He was turned in on himself, and I waited patiently. Houses are a reflection of their inhabitants; they reflect the inner person. How hard and without feeling are the houses in cities where I had lived—how gentle and imbued with love these mountain houses seemed in contrast.

I leaned back and breathed deeply and slowly. My gaze wandered around the modest furnishings of the room. In the middle was a large table on which generations of inhabitants had left their mark. Across one corner was an ancient wooden bench with worn, simple ornamentation. Through the uneven whitewash on the walls I could see the shape and structure of the stones. The aerial of the portable radio, perched on a ledge, had been replaced by a length of rusty, bent wire. The old man sat in front of me, unchanged. There was a feeling of well-being. Every object lived happily with its neighbor. The day's stress fell away like a ripe fruit dropping from a tree. *Yes*, I thought, *the old man can stay silent all night if that is what he wants.* Images began haphazardly to cross my mind but soon addressed more and more the question of why I now found myself up in the mountains in a small house waiting to see if the old man in front of me would let me stay or not. It was up to him.

Then the images took a step backward: I saw the flat fields of my home village, the little stream, the old watermill, fish in a rusty bucket whose mysterious movements I could watch for hours when I was a child. There was my grandfather, that worthy old man. And then there was the tree, the willow standing close up to the railway. A steep bank went down to the fields on the other side of the track.

That tree belonged to me just as so many things in my childhood were a part of me: the beanpoles, the rusty old notice at the railway crossing, and my uncle's accordion, which I would take with me when I went to visit the tree. Shrouded by thick shrubs, I had a great view of the surrounding fields as I sat comfortably on its large protruding roots, leaning against its massive trunk, lost in thought. I could see everything from that spot: the people working in the potato fields, how they spoke among themselves, laughed, or stretched their backs. I played the accordion only when the sound of voices and laughter told me that the wind was in my direction, and then quite quietly so that no one else could hear me. The tunes I played were only for the old tree and myself, and no one suspected that I was watching them or that it was I who could make time stand still, when I chose.

I always went to my tree whether I was happy or sad, but then the storm struck. Yes, it struck, and the next morning everyone in the village was standing around my tree: I could see them all from far off and that was what made it so unbearable. It wasn't so much that the poor tree was lying there and that for the first time I could really take in its huge size—it lay across the rails, reaching the first row of beanpoles and leaving a gaping hole in the ground. When it was alive, no one really appreciated it, but now that the storm had felled it, everyone was standing around gaping at it. That's what I couldn't bear or even understand. The wind was from behind me so I couldn't hear what they were saying. I just stared from a distance — and indeed, I found I didn't want to hear what they were saying. And because I couldn't hear them it was like being in a dream. The pain spread slowly through every part of me, and I stayed until all the people had left.

The wind was such that no one could hear me while it blew across the fields, through the beanpoles, and over the huge hole the roots had left, where I was now able to hide. The gentle tones I coaxed from my accordion that night mingled with the branches and made me unaware of the tears that ran down my cheeks. In the end I climbed out of my hiding place, and when I returned next morning to find them sawing the branches and the trunk into logs before dragging them away, I had come to terms with the loss. I listened to the men laughing as they split the logs into ever smaller pieces: the wood, they said, was no good for burning but fine for lighting fires and firing the laundry copper. I stood watching the faces of these men whom I knew and even liked, and felt I no longer understood them; the way they dismembered my poor tree as though it were of no importance made me say to myself and to my tree, "No, I won't be like them." I said to the tree stump, which was going to be there for a long time yet, "It's no disgrace to be felled by a storm like that."

By now the fire had died down and I was conscious of how late it was. My thoughts swung back and forth between the blurred perception of the room with the old man facing me and the mental journey through my life until this moment. How odd it was to be watching all these events chasing each other and to end up in such an extraordinary place. The events involving the tree had remained vivid for many years, and their connection with my presence with the monk formed an inextricable bond like the links of a chain. What drove me there? Was it luck or the opposite? Was it the yearning of an unformed soul? Or the naïve pursuit of dauntless bravery or eternal joy? Or the questionable courage of the uneducated, who sense a fire laid inside them but have no idea what part to set alight first?

three

I FILLED MY LUNGS with the fragrant air warmed by the fire and leaned back snugly against the stone wall. I closed my eyes and, without any sign of sleepiness, tried to introduce order into my thoughts of past events. I knew that something important was about to set my course away from well-trodden paths into a world that was there but as yet undiscovered. The paths that others had set for me had long since been left behind; I had no choice but to follow a vague track through the time and history of my culture until I reached the old man who now sat, interminably silent, in front of me.

I was determined not to accept that the fractured world I seemed destined to live with was the only one, and therefore at a very early stage I looked for the marks of past times when a great many people had not yet been robbed of their senses. Somewhere there must still be untrammeled joy, unmeasured love, feelings that have not been drowned by sentimentality and souls not weighed down by shelves full of consumer products.

So it was that I was driven to explore the mysteries of ancient cultures, hoping to find what I felt I could not possibly find in my own culture. I was drawn first to the North American Indians, then to the riddles of the lost Inca culture, and like many others, to the meditative strengths of Far Eastern religions—but finally I found myself asking, "Despite their riches, can I really find the truth so far from my roots? Should I not search more diligently in my own culture?" I took this direction, and it was not long before I found two questions that seemed worth further exploration.

The first question was this: Are all the bridges that connect us to our inner beings and to the thoughts of our forebears broken? There must be hidden paths leading us back into a world where people thought of all events and circumstances as parts of a whole. There must be a key to understanding the truths behind our twentieth-century culture a little better.

Then the second question occurred to me: Is it not possible that every one of us contains the seeds from which this understanding can grow again? Is this how we should find the way in?

At first these questions were merely hypothetical, as a practical answer seemed all but impossible. But time taught me that there certainly were answers that would lead me toward worlds I had never thought existed.

Once again I found myself observing the charming austerity of the room. My gaze passed lightly over the bare walls and the shadow cast by the old man. Had I really hit upon a living testimony of those proud people who were known as the "monks of the Teutonic

Order"? Had I now discovered the bridge between my research into the ghostly worlds of the past and a presence in the here and now? Had I perhaps embarked on a dangerous voyage that could lead me astray? Or was I seeing the first fruits of that year when I devoted myself to researching the roots of my culture?

In those early days, the flame of my research was throwing some light on the century of my European culture, but as yet, the beam was too weak for me to see clearly. There were so many questions that still had no trace of an answer, but I was making my first timid steps into the world of the Celts, previously unknown to me. People call these forebears barbaric, but were they? Where did they spring from and what were they like in reality?

Their lives were clothed in darkness and mystery, as was their arrival and supposed demise. An important part of our modern existence must, I felt, be enshrined in theirs. Right from the start I had the feeling that their world held the secrets that I was hoping to find, steeped as it was in mystery and manifested by the power and might of their gods. But why should I lose myself in vague conjectures when there was solid evidence within my grasp? Then and there I decided to follow the traces left by this people until their supposed end, and in this way I discovered a small bright flame in the darkness: I lit upon the mysterious order of the Knights Templar, who combined all sorts of myths, allegorical tales, sagas, and fantasies, inseparable from the mysterious presence of King Arthur, Percival, and the Holy Grail. I was faced with unearthing and grasping the secret, still undiscovered rules of the order, the unimaginable wealth of the members, and their vision of a united Europe. The traces of this mysterious sect are plain to be seen in the cathedrals they built, with methods of construction that evade proper comprehension to this day. Then there is the mystery of the Black Madonna and the many parallels to the rituals and ceremonies of the Celts, and I could not be unaware of the many accusations of gruesome rituals and acts by church or state. Much of the history of these events and this powerful group of people are still shrouded in uncertainty.

I was intrigued by the so-called facts of this piece of history; it was not possible to tell what was truth and what was falsehood; what and who had rewritten parts of it. I was really looking for something quite different, namely the very first signs of this civilization that must also lie in ours. Looking back at this moment I am astonished at how important this little excursion into the past would turn out to be for me, for soon these nebulous studies would become real-life events.

I felt something drawing me to Spain—to the Catalans. I had several friends there, knew the language, and liked the climate, so one day I went to see my friend Jose, whose character is an explosive mixture of fantasy and romance.

We found ourselves in a small bar talking about the legendary Knights Templar and we were wondering how such a small group of people could have assumed such a dominant role in the Western world. We were talking frankly and quite loudly, knowing that we were not likely to move a step nearer to the answer, when something strange happened that had an extraordinary influence on the course of my life. While we were talking I had noticed a man, sitting in a corner of the café, staring silently at his glass. I had the feeling he was listening to us and sure enough, a little later, he stood up and came over to our table.

"Excuse me for interrupting your conversation," he said politely, "but you are talking about a subject that has long intrigued me."

Sitting down, he told us that he was the owner of one of the largest wine sellers in the area. In the middle of the day he liked to take a break from his business and his family, so he was in the habit of coming here for a light lunch. Like us, he had long pondered the extraordinary importance of the Knights Templar, but he had come up with a solution to the enigma. It was based on their relationship with horses.

Silence ensued and I asked myself if this man had drunk too much wine. I admit that I had trouble keeping a straight face so I let Jose do the talking.

He admitted most politely to not understanding the possible connection between the Knights Templar and horses. Horses were the most commonplace of animals in those days.

"Yes," replied the stranger, "but no one understood how to handle horses like the Templars. I know that sounds rather odd, but perhaps if I remind you of the Templars' Coat of Arms—you are familiar with it, no doubt?"

"Of course," replied Jose, allowing a touch of irritation to show through his friendly demeanor. "Two riders on one horse!"

"And do you know why there are two riders?"

"I've heard people say it's because of their inherent modesty—they were happy to share a horse between two."

"But that makes no sense," replied the smartly-dressed man. "The Templars were the richest and most powerful people in Europe; we even know that each Templar would commonly own three horses."

Jose thought for a moment and then asked him to explain.

"The image on the Arms means that the horse bears both…"

"Both of what?" I interrupted.

"Exactly! He bears the man's body and the man's soul, and it is the soul that is most important on this earth."

There followed a pause and then the man rose to his feet, apologized in case he had disturbed us, and left.

We both took a deep breath, ordered another bottle of wine, and continued our conversation in much quieter voices.

In the days that ensued, this strange man repeatedly came into my mind. What indeed was the significance of the two riders on a single horse? It made little sense considering the fact that each rider owned three horses. "The horse bears the man's body and the man's soul" were his words.

four

TIME AND THE EFFECTS OF WINE finally pushed the incident to the back of my mind, and it was not until I happened upon a little book that I recalled the meeting in the bar.

The little book dealt with the symbolism of dreams that was basic to the age-old Semitic culture and how it found expression in these ancient and original texts. On one page I found a piece dealing with the meaning of horses in dreams. The horse, so it said, represented the breakthrough that led to success in battle. This meaning was already concealed within the word, because every letter in the Hebrew alphabet represents a numeral. The Hebraic word for "horse" is *s-u-s*, which has a numerical equivalent of 60-6-60. In all its forms, the number 6 describes a situation in which something new is about to happen. Thus, in the creation of the world, man appears on the sixth day. Good Friday is on the sixth day of the week in which the Crucifixion of Jesus took place, leading to the Resurrection. Then there were the Pharaoh's 600 riders and chariots, chasing the people of Israel who were fleeing from Egypt. So it is the horse with its numerical equivalent of 6 that always appears at critical moments and will appear to herald the end of the world. You make a breakthrough and you achieve victory through the medium of the horse. The horse is the breakthrough; it is the victory.

I have to admit, this explanation hit me with the force of a thunderclap. Like a mantra it kept on repeating itself in my mind: *The horse is the breakthrough and the victory. It announces a coming event of import and that is when it makes its appearance.*

Quite apart from any religious teachings, the similarity of the two recent events fascinated me: the parallel of the claims in the little book and those of the man in the bar who'd said that the Templar's symbol of power was the horse carrying the body and the soul of man—and the soul is what is important in this world.

What a crazy idea that a whole culture should be bound up with an animal. Well, crazy it might be, but I still felt the urge to pursue it further.

First, I reviewed all the information and knowledge about horses that I already had: not much, as it seemed to me, though I was amazed at how many expressions there were in our culture involving horses, such as "to spur on," "to take someone in hand," "to behave in an unbridled manner," "to be on the wrong track," and the fact that we say a gentleman is someone who shows tact and self-control and knows how to regulate his anger and emotions. Furthermore, there is the remarkable event in the history of Europe when women rose to power and influence, namely the mounted Amazons who fought victoriously on horseback. And what about the ancient gods like Poseidon, Greek god of the seas, who is shown riding on horseback on the waves, or Demeter, the red-headed Greek goddess of fertility, or Taranis, the Celtic god of thunder and lightning?

I turned to stories of anthropologists, who clearly state that next in importance to the use of fire, salt, and corn is the domestication and use of the horse. If this is the case, then should we not explore further the relationship between humans and this exceptional animal? That led to another remarkable thought, namely that it is only in Europe that the idea of "man on horse—a rider or knight" has developed. Why indeed was it the horse that was chosen and not some other animal? One thing struck me very clearly: The essence of knighthood in the Middle Ages was not primarily a relationship built on a military need but on a spiritual one. The knights of old are no longer with us and there is not even a true modern equivalent of the concept of chivalry—which represents a spiritual stance based on decency, supporting others in need, having respect for others, and being decent and noble, or, in other words, a truly virtuous person. But even in our modern world there are two distinct concepts of a person involved with horses: an ordinary rider, and someone more in the position of a knight. In old Hebrew there were two words (*farad* and *farasch*), one to describe someone who used a horse as a domestic animal, to be employed for instance in agriculture, and one for someone who forged a rich and rewarding relationship with horses. Language recognized this difference: a "rider" who used the horse for practical purposes and a "knight" who worked on a developing and maturing relationship as a warrior.

If language distinguished between these two states then there must be solid reasons why this should be so, and I became intrigued and excited by the thought that I could dig to the very roots of Indo-European culture and come up with a real living symbol. Then there was the question: Could a horse really help to form a human, and if so, how? If no one were left who could pass on this information, could someone who was prepared to merge his life with that of the horse make the same discoveries that were made by his forebears? Are there secrets that we can learn from horses? Do they have a message for us that could affect our everyday lives? Are they in some way carrying what might be termed a message for us? Yes! That was the question: Do horses have a message for humankind?

five

IN THIS WAY I again found myself being drawn toward the Celts and their neighbors the Teutons, and there were plenty of leads I could follow. For both cultures, the horse was clearly a sacred being as we can tell from its part in ritual sacrifices. There were other animals whose symbols played a part in those cultures but, from what I understood, none were as important as the horse. The information

I held was like a tender shoot but the more attention I paid to it, the stronger it became.

These folk left us very little information to go on except in one place in England, near Westbury, Wiltshire, where there is a hundred-meter-long representation of a horse carved into the chalk hillside. This wonderful white creature only revealed its secrets to me after a number of years' research.

A legend I came across strengthened my resolve in a charming way. It was in the first century AD that a young squire happened upon a herd of wild young stallions. There were nine of them in all, and an old knight encouraged him to take pains in judging them because somewhere among them was the young man's horse. If he chose the right one he would have jumped the first hurdle on the way to being a knight. At first he found that they all pleased him equally, but when he really took the trouble to study them he discovered that one of them was clearly superior to the others. He concentrated his attention on this horse, but the stallion continued eating without noticing him. This was not the case with a small unremarkable stallion, who stood to one side of the herd, pricked up his ears, and never took his eyes off the man.

That evening the knight asked the young man if he had made his choice. He was about to say that he had chosen the horse that was clearly the most handsome, when he heard himself saying, "Give me the smallest of the nine—the one that never took his eyes off me. He's the one for me."

And so they took the scruffy little gray stallion out of the herd and cut off his mane as a token of his new life. In their first few years together neither the man nor the horse derived much pleasure from the other, for the horse was suffering under the young man's mistakes and his heavy hand, his bursts of anger, his ambition, and his unfairness. But as the years passed the young man began to realize that the problems between them were caused by his own actions and not those of the horse, and in recognizing this he began to find himself. Light shone on the dark places in his own nature and at the same time the little gray developed a flawless white coat.

Now that there was perfect harmony and nothing bad between them they returned to the old knight so the young man could receive the mantle of a proper knight. Many years later, history repeated itself with the man's own son: The father took his son to the herd of wild stallions—there were nine of them—and told him sharply to choose his horse with care.

six

THE WIND THAT HAD BLOWN softly during the day now picked up; cold air howled through the cracks in the heavy wooden door. The fire flickered into life again and smoke poured out into the room, seeking a way out. I felt chilled to the bone and it reminded me of when I first took up riding and found myself in a gloomy, neon-lit, damp indoor riding school.

After I had begun to make progress in my research, inside me it was a different story. A fire had been lit—a fire of hope that, through the medium of horses, I could find a way into that world that I had so long been investigating. But I had still not found the quality of life and happiness that the gods and heroes of old spoke of and con-veyed in their songs. What was more, I lived among men who han-dled horses as though they were machines or inanimate objects that could be used up and replaced like any man-made object. Naturally, I spoke to everyone I could find with any knowledge of horses, but in the end I backed away from all of them.

My world was another world. I still observed the people around me—and meant to go on doing so—with the eyes of a child who could halt the passage of time whenever he wished and knew that this world was not the one he wanted. However, there was one thing that reconciled me to others: In spite of the fact that so many people tormented and misused their horses with thoughtless treatment, most of them actually loved them. This knowledge encouraged me to continue with my search. I knew I was on the right road and that, because other people did love their horses, they could be persuaded to change their approach.

I lifted my eyes and gazed at the old monk whom I had so far only addressed as "Sir." Never in my life had I sat so long, waiting in total silence, opposite someone. I considered whether or not to say something but decided not to and let my eyes fall slowly to the floor. My thoughts wandered back to the man I met in the bar—and how I met him for the second time two years later.

On that day he said, in a voice that showed no surprise at meet-ing again, "Yes! I do remember you. You sat over there with a fel-low countryman of mine talking about the Templars and I told you about the role of horses in their lives. Good to meet you again!"

I regaled him with my research and efforts to follow the wafer-thin clues to the story of the Knights Templar but admitted that so far it was like hitting a brick wall when I tried to discover more information about their connection with horses.

"Then I remembered my encounter with you so I came back to find you and ask for your help," I continued.

"How much time do you have?" he asked.

"All the time in the world—whatever is required," I answered.

"Good! Then come back here in a week's time. But I make no promises."

We drained our glasses and took leave of each other only to meet again at the appointed time and at the same small, round table. He seemed to be sunk in his thoughts—even turned in on himself— when I joined him. Without saying a word, he gazed into his glass but then, slowly and without looking up at me, he spoke.

"There is someone who could possibly help you. He's a hermit who lives alone with his horse in the mountains. For many years now he has refused to see anyone at all. He's a difficult fellow, withdrawn, and lives the life of a monk. He meditates all day—not alone, as you might expect, but together with his horse!"

"He meditates with his horse?" I repeated in astonishment. "Does this mean that he possesses the ancient wisdom I am looking for?"

"I can add nothing to what I have told you. I went to see him and told him about you. At first he refused to cooperate but then finally he agreed to listen further. I tried to describe your quest and I do think that there is a glimmer of hope at the end of the road. When I asked him if I could bring you to meet him, he seemed to close up again, but then he asked that you write him a handwritten letter describing what you are looking for. I suggest you meet me here in a week's time, and I am sure by then you will have prepared something."

So it was that the stranger from the bar took my letter to the hermit in the mountains. It was weeks before I heard from him again. Meanwhile I lived through a peaceful, happy time that helped to prepare me for the precipice I was about to come up against. I still treasure the memory.

When a letter finally arrived, I tore it open impatiently. There were only a few words:

"When you come, bring only what is essential. Señor Alda will bring you here. Expect nothing! I make no promises."

seven

I FELT THAT THE NAÏVE YOUNGSTER I had been was now in tatters. Pieces lay on the ground, and I could only hope that something new would be made of them. But was I on the right track? Was there really a secret that horses had been nurturing over hundreds of years or was I following a phantom trail?

I felt uneasy. The tension in me was so great I felt about to burst. The old monk seemed to read my thoughts and my doubts, and broke his silence. He laid his hands carefully on the table in front of him and slowly began to speak.

"Yes, your suspicions are correct. The secret you are looking for does exist. Horses carry their secret with them, whatever happens. It is as if it were written in an almost indecipherable script that only very few people have mastered."

The old man took a deep breath and it seemed to me that it cost him a great effort to speak about these things.

"Mystery shrouds the efforts of those who have tried to discover the meaning of these signs; there are so many ways of searching for the fundamental truths of our existence. Each person can find the way, with enough determination and an iron will, and a chance to pursue this goal without restriction. One of these ways and doubtless an important one in our culture is the confrontation with the being through whom we strive for perfection. But to have a proper understanding of this and be able to grasp the notion with soul and hands is in no way connected with the sentimental notions of so many people who seek their own spiritual salvation.

"Every modest woman down in the village, laboriously carrying out her daily chores while raising her children, gets closer to the truth; every decent peasant and herdsman in the valley gets much closer than those who indulge in meaningless rapture, who abandon themselves to the 'ecstasy of the universe' while suffocating in their boundless vanity."

As if he had shocked himself by his own words, he leaned back and met my eyes for a moment. His expression became distinctly more friendly, which had the effect of making me feel unsure of myself, like a callow youth.

"With horses it's a little like treasure maps: you search here, there and everywhere. Many have searched and few have succeeded in finding anything but those who do find treasure, guard it carefully, just as I would, should if I find one."

Everything about the old monk was enigmatic. One side of his nature is friendly and open and clear, the other side dark, contradictory, and entangled. If someone had asked my opinion of him I would have said, "An odd fellow—I don't particularly like him," and now suddenly I felt as if he were about to send me away again.

"And even if I wanted to explain this mystery to you," he said, "I couldn't do it, so I'd rather not discuss it any more. However, I will certainly talk about what I can and want to do for you. Believe me, it takes a lot of willpower to do so. I'm an old man and my ideas about how to conduct my closing years have taken concrete form. I haven't come across anyone like you before so it's quite a challenge."

Once again the old man's face wrapped itself in thought. Finally he spoke.

"I shall allow you to stay on up here. You won't find very much— just the essentials. More, I cannot say."

While he was saying this, he looked at me with his sharp, penetrating eyes. Any joy that I might have felt was thoroughly suppressed.

"Expect nothing of me!" he went on. "Do not entertain any hopes or make demands on me! And don't thank me: there's little I can do for you. What is possible is that you can do something for yourself. At the moment I cannot tell how this will be but that is why I shall allow you to stay."

I longed to say something, to thank him, to be polite, but I held my tongue. I stood as still as a block of stone, and after a long pause he said, "The cause of today's problems in the world are we humans, and not one of us is free of guilt. The people in the Western world have lit a fire that is out of control and races to the destruction of mankind. Everyone bears some guilt and every bit of guilt is unbearable. And what role do horses have in all this? Isn't it absurd to say they have one? We are speaking of the world's destiny and then bracketing it in the same breath with an animal! Isn't this confusing?"

"Yes!" I said in a voice surprised out of a long silence, "I feel the same," and then repeated myself with more conviction. "I feel the same."

The old man smiled.

"And yet it is the case. Not for nothing was the horse the most revered and holy animal on this earth for thousands of years. It was the companion of the heroes, the gods, and the kings, and often the name of the horse was more famous than the owner. The horse is a symbol of so much—indeed, for many of the qualities that have been expunged from the lives of modern man."

For the first time during the evening the old man leaned forward and came a little closer to me, displaying for once a more human side to his nature. Then almost abruptly, he continued, "Thousands upon thousands think they have made contact with a 'god' but they are as if blinded. Are they not just the same as all the idiots that live in a world that has long ceased to exist? It's as if they have preserved a living corpse for hundreds of years and made it the centerpiece of a gigantic masquerade."

I was shocked by the violence of what he said. I felt ever more unsure about my opinion of this man but nevertheless sat quietly listening to him as he began again.

"And yet many people have an inkling of this other world, expressed in their folk stories, fairytales, and dreams, just like you. Look, I'll open a door for you, but not without giving you a warning. It's not as though you've led an oppressed life; you know you are your own master and so can throw off the shackles that you didn't even know you had. If you do that there's nothing left stopping you. Then you can fly, swim, fall, jump, run, and live without fear; you will forget the fear altogether, for you will be the one to bear responsibility for all your actions—you and you alone. Things move slowly and you have all the time in the world to watch what is going on. Most of the time you will be on your own and will not understand what I am doing or why. It will not be long before you start cursing me just as I have cursed others. You will not have a good word to say about me."

For the first time I noticed how I had gradually jammed myself into a squatting position right at the corner of the wooden bench. I knew I had to stay and see it through even though I longed to leave the place. There must be something vitally important that I could learn from him, I thought. Perhaps the years of being on his own had so twisted him that he could no longer make any distinction between the ancient times and today's world. Was he in full possession of his senses? Was he mad? Neither he nor the man in the bar were much more than strangers to me, but I knew I had to see it through; I knew I was on the right track, even though I had no inkling of the misery that lay ahead for me. His warnings were but gentle indications of what I was to experience and, had I known the reality of the months that lay ahead, perhaps I should not have had the courage to embark on the journey.

Again the wind picked up and scurried across the floor, extinguishing the little flames that up till now had clung timidly to the embers of the once mighty pile of wood.

The room now seemed ghostly and sinister; I was chilled to the bone and my head throbbed with pain. The old man's final words seemed to reach me through a wall of fog.

"…This way of life is a way of trial."

PART III

The Sun Follows Its Course
and the Scents of Nature
Respond to Its Passage

one

IT WAS SHORTLY BEFORE SUNRISE. I stood on the wide plateau above the house. One of the only large trees was behind me on my left. I took deep breaths of the cool, pleasant air and I felt fine, even though I awoke several times during the night. My heartbeat had recovered its normal rhythm. Below me the mist moved so slowly I could barely perceive it, following the course of the valley and revealing the rocky contours of the lake shore. Up here in the hills the day arrived long before the sun made its first appearance. Bit by bit, the increasing light revealed itself in a million little shadows.

In the early hours of the day my mind was clear and unburdened. I tried to put my first days there into perspective.

Before breakfast the old man would go to feed his horse, sometimes going for a ride in the little meadow below the chapel. He had not given me permission to observe him; I had to be endlessly patient. The time would come. In the meantime we spoke little, though it seemed to me that recently he had become somewhat more approachable.

The daily chores now consisted only of work in the house and in the garden. My hands were sore and scratched with the work of carrying the logs I myself had sawed up and split. We hardly ever spoke about horses or their care; I had learned to tread very carefully in my role as guest, and moreover, to stay in the background and not bring myself to his notice by asking irksome questions.

The result of all this was that I still knew little about the man. The picture formed in my mind was painted only by his comments on the various objects around the place and my observations of his habits. An old muzzle-loading shotgun was propped up by the stairs that led up to the three little bedrooms; hanging next to it on two large nails was a rotten old window frame through which his grandfather had shot at intruders. He was badly wounded by them but defended the family successfully and showed a lot of courage. While describing these adventures, the old man's eyes, usually half closed, would open wide with excitement and appear vivid and youthful. In moments like those I felt a growing sympathy toward him and a longing that one day I would find an opening to the spring of knowledge I was seeking. There was also a little cat with gray markings and two dark red milk churns: one that was filled every day for the cat, and another filled only once a year at the summer solstice when, like everyone else in the valley, the old man put out a dish of milk by the front door—this milk being for the elves.

There was also a sword, lying in a velvet-lined case. The old monk had warned in me in no uncertain terms that the sword must never be disturbed, let alone removed. If it were, something dreadful would surely happen. As he said this, he slowly opened his linen shirt, revealing terrible scars that marked his whole torso. During frequent fencing bouts with his teacher, he had often been severely wounded.

In a corner of the room over the bookshelf there was a wooden frame containing a letter from the king, personally addressed to the old man, in which the king extolled the noble origins of the monks.

In a cranny in the wall stood a small wine barrel filled with the heavy, sweet wine that accompanied a standard meal of bread and tomatoes, which we toasted on the embers of the fire. Music came from an old radio set and next to the fire sat a small, blind dog.

As ever I sat there breathing in the smoke-filled air that would soon be renewed with the coming of the day. As I gazed out of the window I watched the rising sun light up fresh green areas on the otherwise barren mountain slopes and bring glimmering life to the dark brown rock faces.

I did not know what the future held, but I knew I was committed to staying the course, however contradictory the circumstances and however tired and weak I felt on occasion.

Night and day a great pan hung in front of the fire. It contained a thick soup that formed the basis of many dishes: with the addition of some ground meal, it even served to make a batter for pastries. Thinned with water from a mountain stream, the addition of some vegetables and meat produced a stew; thickened by the addition of some oats, it became a kind of strange-tasting porridge. Everything was accompanied by tomatoes, bread, garlic, and oil. Fish came from the mountain streams, beef and mutton from local pastures. We sat across from each other at a wooden table, perched on three-legged stools. Lunch was usually eaten in silence—but today it appeared that the old man wanted to say something.

He began by asking me how things were going. I was so taken aback that I blurted out, "Very well, thank you!" and it only then occurred to me that I had wanted to say something quite different.

Then, as if he had prepared what he was going to say, but without looking at me, he began to speak. He did it so softly and with so many pauses that I had difficulty following him, and I found myself leaning forward toward him over my side of the table.

"You can do a lot of things in your life; you can have exchanges and arguments with any number of people—but how can you be certain that what you are experiencing is not illusory? It is indeed one of the greatest dangers that faces mankind: So many are deceived and mislead by false opinions."

At this point in the conversation I was leaning forward with my upper body across the table. My eyes were lowered so that I was only aware of vague shadows in front of me when the old man leapt up and punched me in the chest with such force that I was knocked off my stool and fell heavily to the floor. The breath was knocked out of me; my chest hurt and I was no longer certain as to what was happening.

He helped me to my feet—I found myself exploding with anger, and I pushed him away. Now I was convinced I was dealing with a madman. Gasping for breath, I shouted at him but, given the respect I felt for him, I could not bring myself to truly insult him. However, my whole being seethed with mounting fury.

Meanwhile, as if nothing untoward had taken place, the old man sat down in front of his food bowl, perfectly still and without betraying any emotion. My chest hurt so much I didn't know whether to shout at him, strike him, or bury my head in his robe like a little child and weep.

"Now if that had been a horse's hoof you would be dead, and that is the truth!"

I heard his words with a sense of astonishment. It was the first time he had mentioned horses. In a state of shock from the madness of this unfolding drama, I righted my stool and returned to my place at the table while the old man sat patiently waiting for me to settle down.

Then he went on, as if nothing had happened at all.

"You are about to face many challenges in the coming days, and if you display even a fraction of your usual doziness you won't survive the summer. How do you read the world around you? You have your dreams but you cannot distinguish between dream and real life, between what is fact and what is fantasy. You came here because you are looking for something, but along the way you have engaged in countless situations in which you achieved nothing by dreaming and weeping. You have no alternative but to face reality and truth, and to engage with real conscious life, because the life you are living at the moment is a hair's breadth away from death."

I allowed my left hand, which up till now had been lying on my bruised chest, to fall slowly to the table. I had never before seen this expression on the old man's face. For the first time his words were crystal clear, and sank into my consciousness as if no thought could stop or even slow them.

He stared down at his tightly clenched left fist.

"If my fist—an old man's fist—can floor you, what would happen if a young stallion's hoof struck you? There wouldn't be any more mysteries to discover because you would be aware of all mysteries— in the great beyond."

After a long pause, which I made no attempt to interrupt, he continued, "Everything that I and the horses want to tell you should reach the depths of your being, but how can they achieve that when the way there is gummed up with sloth and ignorance?"

Once again he threw a punch at me, this time in the direction of my face. With lightning reflexes, I raised my right arm in order to catch his wrist, but in the very act of doing so, I knew that he had slowed down his movements so that I had a chance of fending him off, allowing me to learn that such a thing was possible. As before I felt my blood boil with anger, but this time I turned a blind eye. Our arms were pressed against each other, and I was aware of his extraordinary strength, though he gradually eased off as I kept up the pressure. He smiled as he stared into my eyes. Then he reached for the ladle, tipped some of the stew that seemed a little burnt that day into my bowl, and wished me a hearty appetite.

two

THE OLD STALLION LEANED GINGERLY out of his stall to take the piece of apple from the outstretched flat of my hand. His soft lips were gray with a pink patch below the left nostril. The horse's coat was white with a silvery sheen and his friendly eyes were half concealed behind the overhanging main. He seemed completely at ease and displayed all the contentment and dignity of an experienced old stallion. Everything about him suggested a fine characteristic Spanish horse with the exception of his small body size, which hinted at a cross somewhere in his bloodline.

The old man spoke of his horse as though he were a mythical creature. To hear him carrying on about the horse, you would not believe he was speaking about a real live being. When I stood next to the horse I imagined I could feel this glistening aura of unreality and mystery, bestowed upon him by his master. Whenever I knew the old man was in the garden or somewhere in the house, I would go to keep his horse company. The old man was not too pleased about this, and if I forgot the time and was still there when feeding time came around I would be the recipient of some very sharp looks. Although he had never actually forbidden me to be there, he would make his disapproval clear with his curtness and irritability. It's possible that he felt a certain shame at this behavior, more like that of a jealous child than an adult, and when the day's work was done something definitely came over him. I would politely withdraw on these occasions and not give any hint of my feelings toward this lovely creature.

The grounds of the little house had no barriers from the surrounding landscape, which reached far off to the mountains and the horizon. The rocks that had once defined the limits of the garden had long since been absorbed into the undergrowth. I knew every bush and feature around us, but there was one place that was still forbidden to me: the paddock, the sole preserve of the horses, closely fenced about with posts and interlaced branches.

I passed the days waiting—waiting for what? I was not sure, and every now and then it cost me a lot of strength and effort to fan the flames of my hopes. I still could not describe exactly why I was there. Sometimes I had the feeling that I was not an inch nearer to the object of my quest than the day I had arrived and yet I stayed. It was not even that I particularly wanted to stay; it was the result of an ill-defined state of mind that went against all reason, one that I had never before experienced: I could neither describe it nor deal with it.

Occasional exchanges between us kept me going, especially when they developed into unexpected and exciting discussions. However varied their departure points, they always led to the same conclusion: I had to make a change to the state I was in. If I didn't, nothing but nothing would come of it. How the devil he knew this and how he could be so sure of himself I had begun to question. How could it be right, I asked him, to put me down time after time and gnaw away at my courage and self-confidence?

"I know that tomorrow," he said in the end, "the sun will rise. Even if the thickest clouds imaginable cover the sky and I swear at you, the sun will still be there. I cannot cloud over your bright light any more than I can reduce your courage. What I can do is to demonstrate that the night is a place without light or courage."

"Very well, then," I replied. "Can we use that as a starting point? What, in your opinion, can I do?"

There was a long pause before I noticed his features changing—softening in a way that I had not seen before. He put another log on the fire, then said, "I shall withdraw for a time. We shall meet here again at eight o'clock and over the course of the next three evenings I shall try to help you by answering your question."

three

THE THREE EVENINGS THAT FOLLOWED were quite different from any that I had experienced up in the mountains with the old man, and indeed from any subsequent ones. Each night we sat on into the early hours by the fireside, while he spoke almost without pause. Unhurriedly, but with the force of a broad-flowing stream, he painted a picture with his words of the fundamentals of the human condition whose details were ever more interwoven but led always to a unified whole.

On the first evening, the old man spoke about the farmers in the village: He described their work patterns and habits, their needs and their houses, their clothes and their food, even detailing the difference in their usual soup in winter and in summer. I leaned back against the hot stones of the fireplace and never spoke a word. I had eyes only for the old man and pushed everything else out of my mind: why I was there, what had led up to this moment, and what might happen in the future. I concentrated completely on him and now I could see the tenderness in his features and the warmth of his personality as he spoke about the locals or the people to whom he felt most attached, even though he saw so little of them. He was my teacher in that he allowed me to connect with his life, his surroundings, and his being. His words were like a framework that contained the meaning and message that he was determined to get across to me. Between his words and the pauses, images resonated in me and remained with me for weeks, if not months, through all the difficulties I was about to face.

From the body of his thoughts there were certain things that stuck in my mind like needle-sharp splinters, and when I search them out, as I do from time to time, I am beset by the same emotions that I experienced over the course of that evening. Though the old man's experiences could never be mine, I felt I had immediate contact with them, and the understanding of the essence of humanity that had taken root in me allowed me to observe everything around me with new eyes.

Again and again his instruction was finding a bridge into my own world and understanding, a bridge that made a connection between his exotic precepts and my own experiences. He made practically no mention of horses and their message, as if this were much too difficult for me to take in at my present level of understanding. I would have to undergo a good deal more preparation before I could approach that subject and make my way among the hidden traces. The people of that era who were searching for something different seemed all too often like careless wanderers who climb mountains, ill-equipped and with inappropriate footwear—and who don't always return. But all great things, whether ideas or objects, are made up of a thousand small things, and it is only by studying the small things that we arrive at the whole. Many people give up at the first hurdle when they discover the complexity of the small things.

"As you know," he said on that first evening, "the time that human beings have been on the earth is but a blink of an eye. We should remind ourselves constantly of this. Just consider: our earth's surface formed about five billion years ago. Then the continents took shape, and about two billion years ago plants, forests, reptiles, and birds appeared. Dinosaurs disappeared over sixty million years ago, and about twenty million years ago the first apes appeared. It was only two million years ago that our forebears took their first steps. The upheaval caused by what we call modern humanity has really taken place only in the last thousand years, and this has accelerated wildly in recent decades. One does not have to be a prophet to see that humankind will destroy itself before long. It's too bizarre for us really to understand it.

"In spite of all that I have said, I look upon the world with the eyes of a dreamer, of one who still believes against all common sense that the world can save itself. We are standing on the threshold of a new millennium, and I dare to suggest that mankind is in the throes of a huge upheaval in which many people, rather like you, are searching for a new way that will lead them out of the misery of their usual perceptions.

"Life in your era consists of cutting out a tiny part for yourself and ignoring the rest. This results in people seeing the world in the form of a puzzle in which most of the pieces are missing. The tragedy is that they do not see that there are pieces missing, but instead really believe that what they see is the world. Each person sees a tiny part and believes it is the whole."

He went on to describe again the lives of the old men and women in the village, their tasks and their simple nature-oriented way of looking at things, and how they tried to fit all the manifestations of their world into the one they understood. He reminded me about the old shepherd who lived on the west side of the valley and how he trapped fish in the first days of spring each year, scooping them out of the water with his bare hands, to be dried and salted later on.

I felt almost elated by those three days with the old man. They were a blessed pause, a breathing in and a breathing out in the maelstrom of experience that later on would almost drown me. Perhaps his words were specifically chosen to save me from the total collapse, to instill in me a sense of what it meant to lead a simple life and to imbue the idea with legitimacy. That is what I believe now, and it has helped me to understand his strange use of drama that in the end helped me to reach the goals I had set out to find. Indeed it had helped me to go much farther along roads that I would not otherwise have been ready to travel, even had I known they existed.

"If you want to live and survive in any time or world you must never forget the three laws that have been the pillars underpinning life since humans first drew breath. The first pillar is creativity; the second is the right balance or measure; and the third is good energy.

"People today follow ways that ignore all these basic laws; they immerse themselves in their comfort zone and call this 'life.' I could find a quite different description for it..." and he paused a moment before continuing, "more like 'a grim curse.'"

Again he hesitated before calmly going on, "The pillar of creativity is the weightiest of the three. Perhaps there will come a time when you will find yourself within reach...."

His voice trailed off but then he began again.

"Humans are strange beings, even though we are the crowning glory of God's creation. For a start, we seem to have no natural home. Certainly there's one we no longer share with animals: the direct attachment to the forces of nature. In your search for the message of the horse you will come up repeatedly and painfully against this barrier. In the course of human development we have extended the area of our actions and gained greater freedom, but at what cost? The loss of our close connection to the natural world. We have to wear clothes, live in protective dwellings, and cannot survive without fire. We heat our food and feed principally on cereals and grains that we have to cultivate. An animal, by contrast, lives in the immediacy of his world and survives by his instincts. In other words, he is in direct contact with nature.

"Consider humanity! How do we live?"

I looked at the old man without saying a word as he grasped the back of his chair with both hands.

"You see me here in this rocking chair: It is covered in hide, not just because that makes it more comfortable but also because the hide covers a few small mistakes in its construction, for I myself made it. I designed it and very carefully chose the materials. I carried out the work with profound joy and a feeling of inner strength. I put my heart and soul into the process and now I have something to be proud of that I can use. It may not be perfect in every detail but it has a quality that the most perfect rocking chair in the world does not have: it only exists because I made it, and thus it only exists because I exist. If I hadn't existed then neither would this chair, and so it has a value for me that none other could have. It reflects my inner being.

"To be human means having the freedom to carry out an individual creative act and it is exactly this quality that allows us each in our own way to bridge the gulf between ourselves and nature. If you relieve humanity of this possibility or if it is taken away from us by a world in which freedom of expression is held to be less and less important, then we are not only estranged from nature but from ourselves. You could say that, in the most critically important sense, we stop existing.

"We degenerate, with all the resulting consequences for body and soul. We are indeed lost; we have no direction and drown in insecurity. We live without knowing who we are and wander through the darkness not being aware of what our hands are doing."

The old man pointed toward the door with his hand as he continued, "The people down in the valley dance and sing, give birth to children, build their own houses, stitch their own clothes, and make their cooking vessels from the clay they find on the hillside. They speak to the fire and lay rocks in the mountains to mark their fields. They see themselves as part of everything that goes on and they thank God for it. Creative expression is not something given to some people and not to others. All of us, without exception, are endowed with it for our life journeys or we would not be human beings. It all begins with having our own languages, our own personalities, and the ability to express ourselves in movements that are free, harmonious, and either powerful or gentle, as required. Up here we say that every single being is unique, like a star shining in the universe.

"Humans are perhaps the most complex creatures on earth: our sensibilities, our feelings and understanding, and in fact everything that makes the foundations of the first pillar—creativity—is in itself an integrated filigree but also a connected whole. It enables us through constant transformation to find and keep our balance."

While he was talking his gaze had always been focused on something in space beyond the walls but with these final words he looked me straight in the eyes.

"One day you will perhaps realize what weighty consequences these seemingly simple laws hold for humanity. Our existence is a constantly changing process, and in order to maintain a proper perception of it we have to be vigilant and always ready to react. A person who really knows how to live and not be trapped in the concrete prison of anxieties and standards and expectations must exist in a world of continuous change, and in extreme situations has to know the enemy. How can I ever know the real strength of my arm if I have not tested it in a calm atmosphere, free of all anxiety?

"Our skin loses the ability to protect our body from heat and cold when it has not been put to the test and shown that it can survive extreme conditions."

The old man sat up in his chair and leaned toward me. He went on in a clear, strong voice, "There's humanity, with our boundless abilities, living in a world bursting with sensuous riches to be explored, reflected upon and interpreted; there's humanity, seething with fire and natural urges, with our own unique personalities and zest for life! And what do we all do, we wonders of creation? We sit at a desk or a meter-wide conveyor belt; we travel about on an asphalt road or we are confined to a small room that measures a few cubic meters. This is indeed a manifestation of an unnatural existence!"

As if exhausted by this passionate outburst, the old man leaned back in his chair, breathing deeply and regularly.

"And then you appear," he continued, "and want to 'fly,' but before you can do that you have to learn, as we all have to, to finish the puzzle of our quite simple lives. It is only when you see the completed picture that you will appreciate the beauty of the colors and shapes in a way you could never have dreamed." He paused for a long time, just watching me.

"You will have to make a huge step to reach the heart of the truly creative self. If you really want to reach the world of horses and to understand even a little of what they have to tell us, then you must first force an entry into your own world to see what humanity has done to itself. A horse is not going to accept you as a simple body, one of thousands, but rather only in the light of what you do to him."

He rose to his feet, wished me a good night and left. The room was empty. The glow of the dying embers still threw a feeble light. With great care I removed the pelt from the rocking chair and saw that it was well made. I sat in it to try it out, closed my eyes, and fell asleep.

On the second evening at eight o'clock, I sat on a stool with my head and shoulders leaning against the wall of the fireplace, waiting for the old man. Through a small window I watched the sun slowly dipping behind a mountain. It threw a shadow of a wind-curved tree across a slope that stayed for a while as though time had paused. Pensively I watched a bird of prey circling against the crimson sky. What a magical being! I felt for a moment what it would be like to be that bird with the evening wind fluctuating underneath my feathers. I admit I felt a certain envy for this creature that had the thrilling gift of flight. What would be the boundaries of its world? At that moment it lowered its head and stared fixedly downward. I was sure it had noticed something, but had it really done so or was it just playing with the wind, the heights, and its freedom? It inclined its head and the tips of its feathers opened like an exquisite fan as it lowered its claws. Again I felt close to it; I sensed how the gentle, warm air supported it, and then once again the great wings rose above the head of this magnificent gray-white bird. With a single downward thrust of the wings it rose higher, as on a wave, and then remained motionless for a moment of eternity.

"Nothing that bird does is by accident. Its genius is to glide through time and space; it demonstrates to perfection the marriage of an animal's skills to the physical conditions in which it exists. The endless diversity of nature finds completion in art and manifests itself in the smallest details. The smaller the manifestations, the greater the diversity of creation. Where there appears to be nothing, there can be everything. Where there is very little, great things can materialize."

The old man had sat down next to me without my noticing and he spoke so calmly and quietly that I never took my eyes off the bird and watched until it was swallowed by the light of the setting sun.

"Once we have understood this truth then we have made the second step toward understanding. To see these elemental truths at work in time and space: that is the burden of the second pillar. It is the oneness of nature that gives the right balance.

"In the middle of the three windows you can see the sun setting in the west behind the mountains. The little crack in the gable on the other side casts a streak of light onto the curved wall that in the morning moves slowly across it and demonstrates inside the house the movement of the sun. The outside walls show precisely the points of the compass and where certain lines cross and combine to make a circle, which is the very place where we are sitting—here, in front of the fire."

Slowly he rose to his feet, went over to the window and placed his arm in one of the recesses.

"The window is as wide as the length of my forearm and the height exactly three times the length. Here you see three of these windows and when you look at the floor you will observe how the sunlight alternates with the shadows, how the blue lies next to the red and gives the room its form, its rhythm, and this rhythm has the right balance.

"This is how the builders of the past worked when they constructed the great edifices, cathedrals, pyramids, and the sunken cities of the Incas, whose secrets leave us mystified, still defying analysis by any computer. Today no one really knows the spiritual reasons that led to their creation—to the temples and structures of the Celts and other folk many thousands of years ago. These huge monuments bear witness to an understanding of the world and its natural laws that is lost to man today, but they remain the best example of the 'second pillar', the right balance."

The monk calmly seated himself in his hide-covered rocking chair and led me on a journey through his understanding of the way each object was a product of light, balance, and rhythm. He showed me how the same laws applied to music and to the lives of simple folk even though they developed thousands of miles apart.

"This is because in nature everything has the right natural balance and this balance determines the right shape. When in earlier times people changed nature by constructing houses, temples, squares, gardens, and walls they did not consider only the functions of these structures but also ensured that they observed the rules of nature in everything they did. When you enter one of these houses or buildings you are struck with a sense of humility in front of an act of creation that accords with your understanding of nature. Structures like these are for living in and for love. But today we build houses that personify illness, death, and depression, and if you take flight from them you flee into darkness. If buildings do not have a proper basis of balance everything will end in disaster.

"And this right balance is in all that you do and are; in the way you work, the way you breathe, the way you walk and stand, in your posture, in the relationship between your body and your inner being, while you rest and when you are awake, in your actions and in the actions of others that affect you, in giving and receiving, in fullness and emptiness, in excitement and in relaxation. The correct balance is the default setting of nature and must be obeyed if you want to reach for the light and life.

"First you must strive for this natural balance in yourself. You must live in harmony with yourself and so regulate the forces of personal growth. And what about horses? Are they not a worldwide symbol of what we have been talking about?"

The old man carefully added more wood to the fire and I noticed how his movements were all coordinated and smooth. Then after a long pause he began to speak again.

"It's not possible for you to learn all this. You have to feel it; just as that bird seems to break through the limits of perfection, you have to live the experience. When mathematicians study the great edifices built early in the second millennia they try to distance themselves from the mystery of how they were constructed and explain everything in their own terms. In doing so, they distance themselves from the concept of natural balance. Before you commit yourself in your thoughts and objectives to horses, which so wonderfully embody the principles of natural balance, make sure you study the totality of nature. Try to understand how nature went about creating forms, living creatures, and plants—how one thing emerges from another. Make up your mind about everything that surrounds you so that you are free and so that your mind is regulated by nature. Then and only then, will you be living in the correct balance."

On the following day, for the first time I experienced a sensation of security—almost contentment. In these three days we seemed to have established a fragile sense of cooperation so that the upheaval that shattered this the very next morning seemed to come from another world.

On the third evening, we moved on to the third pillar.

"We find the laws of creativity, the right balance, and the correct use of power in all aspects of existence: both in our thinking and in our actions. Their influence," said the old man, "opens up aspects of the human psyche to those who are themselves receptive to everything around them. If you notice only a part of what is going on around you, you might as well notice nothing at all. You have to be aware of everything or you can easily miss something apparently very insignificant that could be of vital importance. Then you will not dig deep enough to reach the essential and end up losing everything.

"The third pillar, the pillar of good energy, is an elemental force because energy simply exists; in its original state it was neither good nor bad. Just as there is light, so there is shadow; there is day and there is night, summer and winter, heat and cold, life and death. Yet all these polar opposites have the same source: both poles of a magnet have the same energy and work in the same way and they only have this energy because the immensity of the universe allows them to behave in this way.

"Power and energy are at the root of our inner being and its workings and therefore embrace light and shadow, life and death. Humanity is the only living species in the world that has the ability to turn one way or the other.

"The consequences of the freedom that humanity has been given are largely ignored today, and the existence of these opposites is in effect denied. Humanity seems to have lost the ability to comprehend them and, being unable to distinguish between them any longer, all too often we choose the easy way out—the way to Hell.

"The pillar of good energy is the one that surrounds you most closely and will therefore be the source of constant challenges.

"If you have already met a challenge presented by either of the other two pillars and overcome it then it is behind you and has served as a good foundation stone, but things are quite different with the third pillar. You have to start again from scratch, always, and if one hurdle is behind you then the next one is already appearing and will be twice as high and dangerous as the one you have just surmounted."

I had my eyes on his face as he watched me like a hawk, and since his words were almost threatening I hesitated before asking the question that was on the tip of my tongue. Finally I took courage.

"And what happens if I stumble over a hurdle?"

After giving it thought, he replied, "With luck you will lose a couple of months or even a year of your life while you find your way back to where you started by a circuitous route. What you learn on the journey should be a warning for the future."

"And if I do not have the necessary luck?"

"Then the best thing for you would be to lose your life."

"And the worst thing?"

"Would be to lose your soul but forced to go on living—a life in Hell."

There was a long silence and then the old man said, "But now is not the time to speak of that. You will be able to feel and identify this energy when the time comes. Anyone that embarks on this journey takes it upon himself to be aware when he meets it. This energy I speak of is everywhere, but when someone comes across it he becomes aware not only of its power but its horror and treacherous cruelty. This is where the road of trial becomes hard and stony, and the more confident a person feels the sooner he meets the next obstacle."

"Is there any way of protecting oneself?" I asked.

He stared into the flames a long time before coming out with an answer.

"The essential is to be strong; that is all that matters—and that you keep awake. Your constant watchfulness will protect you.

"The pillar of good energy will take you along the one road a man should follow and it will take you a long way. But it all starts with what you see in front of you, the seen and unseen elements of your surroundings, and before you turn toward these distant places, including the horses and their secrets, you must learn to distinguish what is good energy and what is not by looking at the simple things around you.

"You don't have to be a genius to understand how nature's energy works since in all circumstances its aim is to support life. It is as if you are following a stream that introduces you to what is beautiful and harmonious; it leads finally to a paradise of abundance and splendor. Let the stream be your guide: it holds the good energy and inhibits the bad. Man has the choice and sometimes chooses one, sometimes the other. Horses can distinguish immediately between them and the moment your eyes wander toward the shadows they will pull you up."

"When nature is working for good, how do you recognize the shadows?"

"Just look about you—everywhere you can see what nature achieves and what it drops. Take this house: once upon a time there were wolves living on this ground, just one of many places where they had their lairs. The ancients who chose this place to build their dwelling knew that it was a place of good energy. Its position in relation to the lake is no accident and the fact that the bedrooms face north is also no accident. The walls and the floors of the rooms are painted in carefully chosen shades of yellow, brown, and white.

"Here people live to a ripe old age because they avoid many of the ills that beset most of the world. They grow old with dignity and keep their faculties and bodily strength until they die. In the fields and in their farms they erect monoliths and towers with stones. This does not have to do with superstition, but rather with their certainty of how to harness the energy of the earth and nature's implacable obduracy. These people desperately want to live and they can only do so if they have at their disposal all the benefits of good energy. Here with us you can see that we practically form an integrated whole with the fire and that we are dependent on the fire for our food consumption.

"All modern rules concerning food consumption have this in common: they acknowledge only the tiniest details of the whole picture and think the rest can be deduced from them, instead of following the example that our ancestors have pursued for thousands of years: first considering the whole and then extracting elements that will be imbued with the energy of the whole."

The old man explained how people in all parts of the world had fed themselves over hundreds, even thousands of years: some were hunters and some were gatherers. Inuit lived off fish, other folk principally from the fruits of the rainforests, and others still from their cattle, but none of them was plagued by the disease of prosperity that afflicts people today. They were resistant to hardship and withstood all that nature threw at them. They all had one thing in common: they knew the unwritten laws of their forebears, what the old man called the "pillar of good energy."

Hour after hour we immersed ourselves in the rituals that humankind followed over hundreds of years to prepare food. The monk expanded on every little detail: which bodily organ was nourished by a particular foodstuff and in what form it was eaten. He spoke in detail about food preparation, describing the ideal shape of cooking pots and the preparation of beans or root vegetables. He was particularly strong on the preparation of vegetables, the simple meat-free diet of the monks, and the effects on the soul.

He concluded with these words: "I've now told you everything I set out to impart. What you have taken in and will make of it is up to you and not to me. Beware of the darkness—you cannot defeat it in open combat, for its weapons are concealed. It is a master of disguise. Many have forgotten how to escape it even though its effects have never been more obvious than they are today. It consumes your fire and your blood, and indeed life itself. It robs the soul of what is most important: the ability to love. Do what you must and what you want to do!

"Go on your way and do not pester me! Look for creativity in everything, obey the rules of the right balance of things, and choose the good energy. Only if you obey this will you survive. And never ask me about horses again if you have not taken in and learned the lessons I have taught you over the last three evenings."

He stood up, pushed back his rocking chair and left, without a word of goodbye. My blood froze and deep inside me I had the first inkling of the grim times that lay ahead of me.

four

DAYS, WEEKS, AND MONTHS slid by and I had nothing to report—not that I hadn't made every effort to put the old man's injunctions into practice. On the contrary, I tried to do so at every turn: I explored form and color in order to understand their deeper meaning. I ate the mushy food and made a sincere effort to find a rhythm in the all-too-similar days that corresponded to the right balance, but all I was left with was a boring, monotonous time that I seemed to be obsessively committed to without the least hope of finding any meaning. Contact with the old man had practically broken off and for several months I just sat on that godforsaken mountain, feeling totally abandoned.

A dark cloud of indifference settled over me and, but for suffering the occasional eruption of pure fury at the old man's indifference toward me, I would have doubted I was still alive. I no longer laughed or even wept. Like a feeble shadow of myself, I simply carried out the few demands of daily life and hoped that I would be left with enough strength and willpower to escape the place. What exactly were these chains that bound me to it?

Even though I had experienced fleeting moments of good energy, I was now feeling flat and exhausted. The day before I was so apathetic that I spent the whole day on the bank of the little river and found myself saying, "Now, I'm going to die." By the end of that day, I felt I was indeed dead.

"The very next time I feel a rage coming on, I'll pack my bag and leave," I said to myself the next morning. "I'll go and tell the old man that I'm fed up to the back teeth with the whole affair. Yes! I'll go today!"

I was sitting with my head in my hands when I sensed the old man in the vicinity. My sensibility to this kind of awareness had become highly strung with all that had happened and I was not mistaken. After taking a few deep breaths, I raised my eyes and looked into the valley. There he was, slowly approaching me. I started preparing what I wanted to say to him and when he was only a few paces away from me, I felt my lips shaping the words, "I have to speak to you. It is important."

"Tell me this evening, if you must! We'll have the time then. For the present, I have to go down to the village and I would like you to accompany me."

What on earth was he up to now? What game was he playing with me? We had never before been down to the village together and now, just when I had made up my mind to leave…. I rested my head on my hands again while the old man waited for my answer. *What should I do?* I hadn't even spoken to another human being for ages and now he wanted me to go to the village with him. I looked up at him.

"Should I put a tie on to celebrate the occasion?" I asked.

But he just stood there without saying anything, and I felt guilty for my outburst.

We sat in silence next to each other in the car as we drove through more populated areas. The sun was shining and the road surface improving by the minute. I held my hand outside the window in the cool air. I had no desire to speak. My eyes were half closed and I just let the sun, the breeze, and the world go by. We passed a girl.

"My God! There are still women in the world," I said.

I was no longer aware of the old man next to me. I tried to imagine what it would be like to speak to her, to ruffle her hair, her skin, to touch her lips, to inhale her odor, to lie in her arms, to gently stroke her breasts, to bury my face in her naked bosom.

The sound of the traffic on the road seemed to come from miles away. My spirit and my thoughts seemed wholly detached from the lifeless body being driven through the little village by an old man in a rickety jeep. Then suddenly it was as if a shaft of lightning struck my body and returned me to the real world. I forgot the misery I had been through and the mushy food when I heard his words: "I've got a horse for you!"

"You've got a horse for me?" I gasped.

"Yes, a stallion. He arrived in a truck from somewhere in the south. He was in a terrible state when he got here but he's been cared for over the last few days. At least we've managed to get him onto his feet. He's a poor creature, that's for sure!"

"A poor creature? Why?"

"You'll soon see."

We drove farther on and I was in a fever of excitement as though the immediate past never happened. The road turned into a narrow, bumpy lane before we stopped in front of a dwelling where a wizened little man opened a door and spoke a few words to the old monk in a dialect that I did not understand.

"Follow me!"

We went through a darkened barn that the sun hardly penetrated and there in the distance I caught sight of a silhouette. A little closer and I could discern a somewhat black, weak-looking, bony creature with its head lowered. Surely this was not the animal he had found for me? I kept on hoping that it would all change, that one of them would say, "Don't be anxious! Of course this is not yours. Your horse is over there."

Instead, I heard the old man saying, with a touch of pride in his voice, "He's a genuine Valenciano!"

All the misery of the recent past as well as the vision of the girl we saw on the journey reared up into my consciousness. I could feel the beads of sweat forming on my forehead. *The world is going round without you*, I thought. *It must all be a dream.*

"So," I murmured, "a real Valenciano."

I took one step toward the stallion, which still looked like a paper cutout against the light, but as I approached he lunged at me with bared teeth and crashed against the wooden railing and the iron posts. I sprang back—at least I had learned something in the mountains—and knock the two old men out of the way.

"As I said, he's a proper Valenciano. He's killed two men, a mare and a foal. He's a real devil and his life has been a hell on earth."

All I wanted to do was get to sleep. On the return journey we spoke not a word. When we got back, the horse was fed and seen to. I went to bed but woke in the night, the light still on, as were all my clothes. I undressed and only woke up late in the morning to find the sun shining and a horse in the garden. My horse! A proper Valenciano!

five

BY THE END OF THE DAY, I hadn't seen the old man. I had a dreadful headache and a sore throat and felt stiff all over. I spread an old horse blanket on a flat rock sticking out of the ground so that I could keep an eye on the garden below. Someone must have brought my horse—Yes! My horse!—up early in the morning.

The afternoon sun cast a sharp light on the south face of the house, in front of which there was a small garden surrounded by a stone wall. A gap where the stones had crumbled was crudely blocked up with pieces of wood and the odd rock, and that, for the time being, was all that had been prepared for the horse. The parched earth provided a few clumps of green for the horse to nibble on, but nothing like enough to sustain him, so I prepared a bucket with a good portion of alfalfa and water. I tipped it over the low wall where the stallion was looking at me with laid-back ears and bared teeth. Then I took a quick step backward and watched him while he greedily ate his food without dropping his aggressive stance.

It had been an unbearably hot day and I didn't think I had ever seen so many flies and mosquitoes, but instead of retreating to the coolness of the house I sat there wondering how on earth I should make a start with this unpromising creature. The more I looked at him the more hateful he seemed with his half-starved, caved-in flanks, his prominent barrel-shaped rib cage, his outthrust shoulders, his bony, sunken back, and his long, thin, unshapely neck, which supported a head that looked more like a ram than a horse and deep-set eyes under hollows. If that was not enough to put me off I only had to look at his dull, unkempt, matte-black coat, flecked with white age spots.

I still felt the possibility of compassion toward him, if only he would allow it, but he seemed to take amiss any approach on my part by laying his ears back and baring his teeth. I wondered how on earth they ever got him up there.

The dull, afternoon hours dragged by, and I did not notice the old man's return. It was only when I went into the house that I found him sitting in his rocking chair, reading a book. He said hello in a friendlier manner than was his wont as I walked past him into the kitchen to prepare something for dinner. However, when I called out to say it was ready, he had disappeared. He returned sometime later and suggested I put some water and feed in my horse's stall.

"What stall?" I asked. "We haven't got another one."

"I've led him up to the old deer house," he said in a calm voice. "He'll be protected from the cold and the wind during the night— and from the rain as well."

"You led him up to the deer house!" I said in astonishment.

"Yes, just that!"

"However did you manage it?"

The old man made no reply, so I repeated my question: "Excuse me if I seem to be inquisitive, but please tell me how you managed to do that when this devil of a creature attacks anyone that gets near him."

"It's not a devil of a creature; it's a horse," he said.

"You're right, of course, but from what I have seen he attacks anyone and anything that gets anywhere near him. Do please tell me how you did it. After all, that is why I am here: to learn from you."

"I see; is that so?" is all he said in reply.

I breathed slowly and deeply to keep down my rising anger as the old man went on in his calm voice without even looking at me.

"Yesterday you said you wanted to speak to me. Now's the time if you want to."

I gazed at the cracked plate in front of me but could find no words for a long time. When I had calmed down, I said, "It seems that you have a way of mastering this horse. Toward me he behaves like a wild beast, but clearly not toward you. How do you do it?"

"This is what you have to find out."

"And you are not going to tell me."

"No!"

"I have to work it out for myself?"

"I don't know, but I fear it's the only way forward."

"And if I get killed?"

"Then at least you have had a few nice days up here staying with me!"

I was speechless. I rose to my feet and went out to take the water and feed to my horse.

six

THE NEXT MORNING we built an enclosed area for the horse on the south side of the little house that reached as far as the edge of the cliff where the rock face dropped a good thirty feet. We constructed the fence with quite thin wood and when it was finished I thought it was the neatest wooden fence I had ever seen. Not a single piece of wood fitted exactly but that was what I liked about it. It made me feel good.

The old man left; I took a deep breath, stretched out on the ground and made myself comfortable. I had the feeling I had won a little freedom.

I knew the old man was unlikely ever to enter this place so I had a feeling it was mine. The frontiers were the fence, the side of the house, and the cliff plunging down into the valley; they delineated my own space and gave a different feeling to the whole plateau.

I sat down on the dusty ground and looked at my horse. I had the feeling that he looked different today: not by any means beautiful, but strangely changed. I almost felt a touch of emotion as I spoke to him.

"So, old thing, you're a Valenciano! I don't have the least idea what a Valenciano is but I shall call you Vali, and if you will agree not to attack or bite me then we can spend our days together, and I won't be so lonely!"

In all my time in the mountains this was one of the few moments when I felt a breath of contentment and for a few weeks the wish to leave the place evaporated.

The old man had never seemed to be that interested in me, but from that point on my interest in him also diminished. I only saw him at mealtimes and not always then, because quite often I gave them a miss and sat by the paddock or conscientiously mucked out Vali's stall. It had been ages since I had asked anything of the old man but, happily, he had finally told me about Valencianos, describing their origins with this legend:

"In the Middle Ages, a group of riders once met up in the town of Valencia. They made a stop in the vicinity of a stable whose owner had the reputation of having a good understanding of horses, as well as profound knowledge of the art of healing. It happened that one of their horses was ill at the time so the owner of the stable took the horse in hand. It was not long before the horse showed signs of improvement even though he kept to his stall for some days in a weak condition. The owner of the horse approached the man and said to him, 'You have undoubtedly observed the bony and unrefined body of this horse; it might surprise you to know that you couldn't find a tougher horse in the whole world though this breed is unknown in your country. Time is running short for me; I should be on my way but I would like to offer you this horse as a present for your kindness. I have a feeling you will have the ability to tame him.'

"'To tame him?' asked the stable owner.

"'When he is well and his legs are strong again you will soon find out.'

"The stable owner thanked the man warmly and saw him on his way.

"When the horse recovered from his illness he turned into the most stubborn and intractable creature the stable owner had ever come across. However, the owner was sufficiently impressed by the horse's courage and toughness to decide to put him to stud. And so from that day to this, horses are born that are bony and black, with heads like rams and quite unlike any others. Their most distinctive characteristic is an unbending spirit. This is the horse we call a Valenciano."

seven

ONE DAY FOLLOWED ANOTHER and brought a certain calm, but whereas at first I was very careful and not a little terrified when I brought Vali his food or mucked out his stall, in case he had thought up some new trick to make my life a misery, I later became increasingly frustrated. Any hint of sympathy that had taken root in the early weeks had completely disappeared. I had at first entertained the hope that our daily encounters would lead to an understanding but it was not to be. His attacks rose in intensity as in frequency, and he gave the appearance of relishing my discomfort and of using me as a whipping boy. My feelings of desperation at my inability to cope ate into my spirits.

This mounting anger toward the horse was matched by similar feelings toward the old man. Could he not have helped me? Of course he could, but he chose not to. I could hear myself swearing and my teeth snapping together in fury, and when I was alone in the mountains I was consumed with shame and feelings of inadequacy. What I was doing was the opposite of what I had intended, and every time I grasped the stick that I kept nearby for protection I knew the poison of despair and hatred was consuming me.

One day I could bear it no longer. I sprang over the fence; Vali stood still. I swung my stick above his head but the situation was soon reversed: he was on top of me and as I collapsed under his weight I stopped breathing. The next thing I knew was that the old man was kneeling beside me, my lungs were burning, and I was struggling to catch my breath.

I heard the old man saying, "If he had bitten you, you would in all probability not be alive. But at least he now knows precisely how weak and pathetic you are!"

Days and weeks passed. Full of frustration and shame, I did only what was essential in Vali's stall. I walked in the mountains, weighed down with melancholy. I thought of my past life, my youth, my laughter, my loves, and all the times I had been full of good spirits and energy. It seemed an age away that I had lived that previous life. The sun followed its course, the light and the air and the fragrances around me changing as it traveled across the sky, but for me life had stopped moving and I was drowning in self-pity.

I couldn't go forward or back and the hole I had dug for myself seemed bottomless. I staggered from day to day like a man in fog, overwhelmed by hopelessness. I hardly ate any more. I had reached my limits, my final frontier.

At the very moment when everything seemed hopeless, the rhythm of my life changed again. It was as if destiny had enjoyed reducing me to the lowest possible state when flight was all that was left to me and then, at the last moment, turned a page in order to stop me, only to repeat the same game again.

My frustration had sprung from the fact that Vali was my sole companion so often and yet he rejected me out of hand—but one morning as I approached him, I could see that something had changed. He wasn't eating and didn't appear even to see me. At first I ignored it, but when his behavior remained strange I feared he was suffering an acute attack of colic. When I alerted the old man, he replied, without even going to see the horse, "He hasn't got colic."

That was all he said, so I had no choice but to keep watch on Vali throughout the day.

In fact, he didn't have colic, though his condition seemed to me to get worse by the hour. If I approached him slowly, his aggressive reactions were ever less severe than I had learned to expect. By the end they had almost ceased: he allowed me to lift his feet and groom him without a problem. What had been denied me in the previous weeks had now been handed to me by illness. For the first time I had bodily contact with my horse without danger. As a result, I now spent hours in his company. There seemed to be no improvement in his condition, but I could not help thinking how important this creature had become in my life, without being able to explain why.

Once again I sought the old man's advice. This time he came with me and carefully examined the horse's eyes, his teeth, and his ears, and then after a long silence he said, "There's nothing I can do. It's part of a process. Keep watch over him! That's all I can tell you. Keep watch!"

eight

SO I SAT BY VALI'S STALL. I shared his suffering. He ate less and less. In the end I hadn't the wish to go and see him. After all, he was an old horse and probably his symptoms were due to age.

Day followed day and his suffering seemed to increase. The inside of his nostrils and his gums were bright red. He had a fever and when he drank a little water there were the strangest noises.

The water gushed out of his nose while he coughed and choked in a manner I had never come across before.

I fed him some garlic and led him out into a lusher area of pasture and there was nothing he wouldn't allow me to do. He no longer snapped at me or in any way attacked me; it was as if he was in another world and had left his lifeless body behind. In short, he was a picture of misery.

In the end I could bear it no longer. I shouted in his ear, "Fight, man, fight!"

I even found myself wishing that he would recover enough of his old feistiness to attack me again—anything that showed a sign of life. After all, if he died what point would there have been to our meeting each other?

One day it was raining while I stood listlessly in Vali's stall. Suddenly the old man appeared.

"How is he today?" he asked.

"How is he? How is he? How do you think? You can see how he is. Why do you ask me? It seems to me you couldn't care less what happens to this horse. Would you sit back and do nothing if it were your own horse that was as ill as Vali? I thought you were a horse lover—someone who understood horses. If you are, then can you do nothing to help him? If it were your horse, I'm sure you would."

The old man stood listening without saying a word and then very quietly, as he turned to go, said, "But it's not my horse that's ill. It's yours."

I simply did not understand him. Indeed, I hated him. I hated the very way he had said that. I thought I even detected a sarcastic little smile on his face as he said it. Why had he abandoned us like this? Was it all in order to torment me—or indeed both of us?

At dinner, there we were again sitting silently facing each other. Then suddenly he said, "After you have put your horse away for the night, come back and see me. I want to speak to you."

Though I considered what to do for a long time, in the end I did as he had asked.

"Here I am! Fire away!" I said.

"You want me to help your horse."

I made no reply.

"Your horse cannot be helped. He's not ill."

"You don't say! You mean I'm making it all up?"

"One could almost say that, yes!"

I sprang to my feet and made as if to leave but the moment I turned my back on him, I felt a sharp blow on my neck that tipped me back onto my chair.

"You stay here! You've been running away from things long enough. Now listen to me!"

I had never seen the old man's face like it was at this moment. He was quite changed. I even felt afraid of him.

"I've warned you often enough. I can no longer watch how your horse suffers from your self-satisfaction and your wretched behavior. No, your horse cannot be helped because he is not really ill. He shows all the signs of the illness in you, deep in your soul. That is what he is trying to tell you about! But you are blind to anything that does not flatter your wretched vanity. You have eyes only for yourself and your own problems. Not for a single moment does it occur to you to try and master your boundless egoism. This horse of yours is not any old horse. He is special. He is better than you could possibly imagine. You haven't the least idea. Not an iota!"

I sat as if struck by lightning and thought, "He's right." I lowered my eyes, indicating I was prepared to listen to him. There was a moment's silence and then he began to speak in a calm voice.

"Have you ever taken the trouble to look into his eyes? Have you noticed how watchful and intelligent they are? Have you noticed how delicately the tips of the hairs inside his ears point downward? And how well the ears are positioned, so small and strong? Have you for even one moment noticed how excitedly his nostrils tremble? Of course not: you are immersed in your own misery, in your wretched self-pity over your fate and what you consider your misfortune in being stuck here with a worn-out old horse. What you yearn for is a fiery young stallion, and so you have essentially rejected this creature that totally depends on you. It is this that accounts for his condition because you are his whole world. What makes you think you have the right to impose your misery and your oh-so-dreadful fate on him? Do you understand that it is you and you alone who are to blame for his condition?"

I sat, staring at the floor between my feet. Nothing was said for some time but then he continued, "Have you ever looked into the face of a mother holding her dead, bloated child, bloated from starvation, when she no longer has the energy to express a fraction of her misery? That is an example of true misery, and a person in her state has the right to complain. But think about the people back in your world: look at how they moan and complain, how greedy and overfed they are; how they carry on about the slightest misfortune; how they lament the fact that they have not won the lottery, that they didn't succeed in taking home that woman from the bar, that they found a scratch on their car's paintwork or lost a gold ballpoint pen, or that the neighbor's child woke them up by crying at midnight—that their spouse kissed someone else and their son failed his exams, that it's raining or too cold or too hot. They complain for the sake of complaining, and if they don't do it aloud, it is inside them, turning into a cesspool of hatred, greed, and wretchedness.

"Well? Do they learn or do they dig themselves even deeper into the illusion that one day some event will change the course of their fortunes and relieve them of their wretchedness?

"Suppose that one day they win the jackpot. Someone who wins the lottery usually discovers that it is the last great illusion and finds no happiness as a result. And should they win it, they would complain even more because now they are worried about losing it. A man might find the woman he had been longing for: she's pretty, elegant, and smells like a bed of roses. What does he do? He torments himself with the fear that she will leave him.

"Grief, fear, and concern for their pathetic selves have so thoroughly taken them over that they are no longer capable of judging the truth of their actions and their consequences. Life is passing them by—as is the beauty of this world—and the same applies to you and your horse. To make matters worse, he's now sick and I am supposed to help him. What medicine would you suggest?"

I rose slowly to my feet, went outside, and gazed into the silvery night sky. When I returned, the old man was still sitting in his rocking chair, reading a book. I stood in the doorway for moment and then asked quietly, "Is there anything at all I can do?"

He let the book slip onto his chest.

"Have you forgotten everything I told you? Have you at least remembered about the three pillars of wisdom? There's a lot you can do. You can still think, and you are still capable of feeling emotions. For the time being you cannot do anything and there's no point in fooling yourself. What you can do is notice what effect your attitude and your handling has on your horse. If all you can say to yourself is, 'My horse is old and mean; I am weak, alone and unhappy,' what on earth can you expect? Well...sit down!"

Very unsure of myself, I walked across the room and sat down in the place I chose on the rare occasions that the old man agreed to talk to me. He looked at me for a moment, leaning forward to speak.

"For God's sake, man. Try to understand a little of the meaning of this world! Thought precedes and engenders actions and states: if you allow yourself to be sad, what result other than depression can your state produce? How can your horse resist this condition for any length of time? He will inevitably be dragged down into the morass. And what other results might stem from this? What other fruit will sadness produce? Well, it's clear we have to get out of the morass as soon as possible or disaster will result. We must not let this happen, so we have to summon all our strength and willpower to gather our forces and center ourselves.

"You have to open your eyes; for a start, look at me. Look me in the eyes!"

I looked at him.

"Do you see me?"

I made no reply.

"I asked you a question. Do you see me?"

"Yes! I see you!"

"Why can't you thank God that you do, that you have eyes and can see the world around you? The way you are, you might as well be blind. Answer me!"

"Yes! I might as well be blind."

"Thank your God that you aren't!"

I said nothing.

"Thank your God that you are not blind, I said."

"God, I thank you that I can see."

"Good. Now stand up!"

I stood up.

"Have you got strong legs that allow you to walk?"

"Yes!"

"Then…."

"Yes, okay, okay, I thank God that I have healthy legs and can walk."

"Good! Are you hungry?"

I sat down again and replied, "I thank God that I am not hungry and that my stomach is full."

"Are you unhappy?"

"Yes, and I thank God that I am unhappy!"

"No, no, no, you nutcase!" he shouted. We both laughed and I thanked God that I could laugh again and feel some sympathy toward the old man.

"Well, now it's your turn and we'll leave God out of the equation for the time being. We've got to change pace and find the opposite of your past state. How would you describe that?"

"I'm happy and strong!"

"Good! That's a start. Now repeat after me: 'I shall do everything in my power to be happier, more contented, and stronger.' Go on! Say it!"

I obeyed the old man.

"Is it working? Don't laugh! I mean it. We have an obligation to the world, so try always to direct your thoughts toward the light and good energy! You have to concentrate your thoughts on the positive aspects of existence. This is your schooling and you will become a living witness to the energy that is now being poured into your being from all sides. This does not mean that you have to lie to yourself, but you can now open doors into a different future, as you can for your horse.

"Look through the middle of those three windows at that little stunted tree, leaning away from the valley as if it has grown crooked in order to avoid the slope. We see nothing and yet the wind touches everything between heaven and earth, day after day and without cease. We see nothing and yet the wind leaves its mark on everything. That little tree is an impressive witness to the way the wind has blown for many a year. Everyone can understand the wind's unchangeable nature.

"You ask me what you can do. Just that! Be like the wind that never ceases to blow over the slope of the mountain and organize your day's work in the same way. You have to be strong, particularly if your work does not achieve immediate results. It's as if you decided to cultivate an arid, abandoned field. You have to carry water from a great distance and when you pour it on the ground it disappears. Not for a moment do you get to enjoy the sight of the water on the dry ground.

"You perform your daily, thankless task without the least hint of a result. Your hands are covered in blisters as you sit staring at your field month after month. Just when you feel like giving up, the rays of the setting sun catch a tiny glimmer of something green. You are roused from your lethargy and you look at it from several angles. It's not an illusion! It's real, and you see that while you were staring at the dried surface of the field and giving up all hope, a miracle was unfolding underneath the surface.

"Now, with renewed energy, you fetch water to encourage, nurture, and protect this sign of life that you have enabled to become a reality, this living creation that, without your help, would still be dormant. Go and do your work—and do not expect a reward! It will arrive when the time is ripe. Do not think of the end product, for that will come, too. Only concentrate on the daily interaction with your work and be aware of *how* you work. Be grateful and devoted, and let all your observations be sincere and appreciative of beauty in all that you do. Do not try to do other things. Just concentrate on the task in hand and treat everything that happens as a gift.

"For the time being that is all I can tell you. See how you get on!"

I went out to my horse and greeted him, "Well then, you young elf. You fit-as-a-fiddle bastard!" I laughed with all my heart and soul, and I stroked him affectionately.

nine

IT WAS QUITE A FEW WEEKS before my horse's demeanor improved. In the meantime, my feelings of misery dried up but were not replaced by happiness, just emptiness—stark emptiness. The more I tried to follow the old man's recommendations, the more my efforts trickled away into nothingness. My horse's illness had brought me a little closer to him, but now that his strength was returning little by little, so was his aggression. Very little trust seemed to remain and whether any contact would be possible now depended entirely on Vali's mood. Should he attack me once again and try to harm me, I would be helpless.

My relationship with the old man seemed to have changed as well but once again not as I might have hoped: his apparent lack of interest in me seemed to have turned to contempt.

I therefore decided that I would make no further effort to improve my relationship with Vali. It was clear to me that I had reached the end of the road and that there was not a grain of hope left. This in itself did not upset me, though occasionally I felt myself slipping from a state of emptiness to one of fear.

More and more I felt the life force draining out of me. Not only had I failed to find what I was searching for, I felt I was losing what I already knew I possessed. I was no longer homesick, nor did I miss other people. The summer sun no longer seemed to warm my skin, nor did its light with its energy affect me.

Then one warm, humid evening when my shirt stuck to my skin and the weather showed no signs of breaking, we sat at the table as the sun dropped between the mountain peaks. I was staring, sunk in my thoughts, at the stone wall opposite, whose crags and crannies were playing a tune with the gentle rays of the setting sun, when the old man began to speak. My body tensed as if it feared another onslaught that it would not be able to withstand.

"I have no choice," he began. "I have to say something to you."

A long pause ensued. I could hear his labored breath and, in spite of his calm appearance, I could sense the inner turmoil.

"I think I made a mistake when I invited you to come here. I consider you to be in a state of unparalleled weakness and sickness. It takes all my remaining strength not to fall ill myself. It would be best for both of us to part."

I rose to my feet and left the room. I felt as if the blood had drained out of my veins, as if any remaining life force had been torn out of my body. I staggered to my room, tumbled into bed and tried to forget everything: life, death, my horse, and myself. When I awoke I was bathed in sweat; my heart was beating feebly, I couldn't think, and everything was in a muddle. There was a pressure deep in my stomach as though I might be sick. My breath was short and shallow. I got up, stumbled toward the door, tore it open, and fumbled my way along the dark corridor and down the stairs. I took a turn that I had never taken before and ripped open the door to the room where I knew he slept.

I shouted into the darkness with all my remaining strength, "I know I'll never find what I came for, what you think you have possessed for so long, but there is one thing I will never lose and that is my dignity." My voice rose even higher in tearful desperation. "Yes! I'm leaving and I shall find my own way without your help!"

I struggled back to my room. Then all was still and I slept like a log until morning.

When I woke up, I went over to the window and looked out into the valley. The memory of the last night's events slowly returned but without any anxious feelings. I felt a deep sense of calm, not a trace of fear, and I was sure that everything would be all right. As I gazed at the landscape it seemed to me that something had changed: it was as if I were looking at it for the first time. It was beautiful in a way I had not appreciated until now. Deep inside me I felt a wave of emotion.

From my vantage point I could see most of the farm and I couldn't help noticing first that the jeep was not where it usually was, and secondly, that Vali was not in his paddock.

Strange, because at this time of day he was always there, waiting at the fence for his feed. I went outside but could not find the old man. The sun momentarily blinded me as I looked into Vali's stall, but when the glare was gone, I saw that it was empty. I was quite sad. It was as if I had already said goodbye to him. Well, I thought, that's how things come to an end.

I wandered back to the house and even though I couldn't quite get my thoughts together, I was calm. I went back to my room to pack my few bits and pieces and as I came down the stairs, I heard a car coming up the hilly little road to the property. *It doesn't matter what he says to me*, I thought. *I'll take my leave in a friendly manner.* I opened the door and there he was coming toward me, but behind him the jeep he had arrived in was not the one I knew. He came straight toward me, holding a map in his right hand, and I couldn't help noticing that he looked twenty years younger. He even spoke in a voice I hardly recognized.

"Have a look at this map," he said, holding it in front of me. "This is where we are. Up here by this red line, you will find a herd of wild horses. It's no easy job finding them as there aren't any tracks leading to where they are and not a soul living nearby. You're a free man and you can come or go as you please. If you choose to stay with the wild horses, don't come running back when you're cold or hungry or think you are about to kick the bucket. Only come back when you are sure in your mind that you should. I'm a poor man with not much more than you but I want to give you this car as a present. Go and find the horses and see how things turn out for you!"

My God, I thought, *so it's not all over!* That's all I could think of: *It's not over yet.* My knees were trembling as I took my leave. I felt light-headed as I roared out of the yard—and happy. Yes, I had said a quiet farewell to the old man, so quiet that the words were barely audible.

"*Gracias, hombre, gracias!*"

PART IV

....

He Is Not There to Carry
Man's Grief

one

THE SUN WAS SHINING. Yes! I was aware of it again. I had my old radio with me and persuaded it to produce a couple of barely audible songs that I even accompanied in a voice weakened by all the recent events. The sadness had taken its toll on me and I only hoped that I had not left it too late to break free.

My route took me northward even farther up into the mountains, heading for a little village that I had heard about years ago. Apparently a handful of young people had gone to live there, hoping to carve themselves out a new life and to restore the ruined buildings. I saw that where I was supposed to be heading was not far from this hamlet. The sun was beating against the side of the mountain that my serpentine road was slowly climbing until I came to a tiny village inhabited by only a few people.

Most villages up here had long been abandoned. The result was a secretive atmosphere that I wanted to investigate as I passed through them, wandering along the deserted streets and trying to understand what the lives of the people who had lived there were like. This village, however, although dilapidated, was still sparsely inhabited, and there was even a bus stop. I noticed a few signs of life such as a child's plastic toy lying on the pavement, a bright window blind behind a window railing, and washing hanging on a line across the street.

Voices came from the doorway of a bar, so I entered and found myself in a cool, shady interior. The floor was strewn with cigarette ends and pieces of paper. Two old men sat at the bar; I greeted them in a civil manner and sat myself down at a small table in the corner where I could take in the atmosphere of a place that had once been thriving and was now almost dead. I accepted the food I was offered and ate it with gratitude and the little pleasure I was still capable of feeling. When I had finished, I asked the waitress about the village inhabited by the young people. She knew where it was but said it was too complicated to explain how to get there and that there were no signposts. However, at midday a bus would come from the village with one or two of the inhabitants who had pottery and home-baked bread to sell. With the money they earned, they would buy necessities that were not available in their small community.

When I learned this I knew I had only to be patient. I sat on a bench at the edge of the village in a little square next to a stone fountain where two children were playing in the pleasantly warm autumnal sun. After all I had been through, I began to believe I had once again entered the real world and, watching the children play, I even felt homesick—but for what?

I had abandoned the place where I had been so unhappy over the last few months, but what was left of the person I had been before? I was a changed person; I could tell that from the way I perceived people and how I engaged them in conversation.

In the end the bus arrived, a worn-out, noisy vehicle, from which two elderly ladies and a younger man and woman emerged. The young woman was wearing plain-colored trousers and sturdy shoes. I went up to her and enquired about the village.

"Yes, I'm from there. We can go up there together, if you are taking your car?"

"Ye…es!" I said hesitatingly, but we were soon deep in conversation. Her name was Paloma. She told me about life in the village and how she never wanted to live anywhere else, though she still had the idea of making a trip around world. I liked Paloma: she was quite short and a little plump, with a friendly face and a wonderful laugh. As we drove along the mountain road, birds of prey circled overhead throughout the journey. With the old jeep in a low gear we crept up the narrow, dusty, winding road for at least half an hour, when suddenly, as if out of nowhere, there was the little tumbledown village, sitting on a plateau with an astonishing view into the far distance.

Meanwhile the sun had set and the villagers had all gathered round a large table in one of the houses. I was no longer thinking of my horse or the old man or the miserable loneliness of the last few months.

On the walls, an attempt had been made to disguise the crumbling plasterwork with light blue paint, and in the flickering light of the flames from the huge open air fireplace the pale blue color produced a feeling of pulsating life. When everyone else had left, Paloma and I sat alone by the fire, gazing into the flames and talking. She had a kind and tender nature. Her home town was Pamplona but she came here whenever she had the time, either hitchhiking or in one of the rickety buses.

"I love coming here," she said. "I help with gardening and do my bit. I can learn a lot from these folk: they make as many things themselves as they can. I take home the earthenware pots that I make and fire here."

Then it was my turn to tell her about the horses and the ideas, by now almost lost, that had been driving me on. At this distance it seemed so absurd and out of touch with ordinary life that the more I tried to explain it to this good woman, the more removed it seemed from reality. I had the strange feeling that real life was knocking at the doors of my being and saying, "Wake up, man, you've been dreaming!" From dwelling on these thoughts I again became conscious of the flickering candle flames and the dying embers of the fire; of Paloma's sweet-smelling fragrance, her dark red velvet dress, and her lovely, wavy hair. Oh yes, and there was the white of her blouse.

It had begun to turn a little cold—because the door to the balcony was broken—when she said, without losing an iota of her honest, open nature, "You'll sleep with me, won't you?"

With a little intake of breath, I replied in a quiet voice, "Of course!"

"But for me, it's a change! Normally I only sleep with women."

"You must be joking!" I replied.

"No!"

I stared through the broken door at the star-filled heavens and I laughed. Yes, I laughed, and in that moment it was almost as if my recent tribulations with the old monk had not happened.

two

WHEN I WOKE UP my feelings of anxiety had returned, as they always did in the morning. I was lying on my back, naked, with only a thin woolen rug for cover. Paloma was cuddled up to me, her soft hair brushing my face, and we were a little damp where our bodies touched. I began to breathe deeply and slowly so that my feelings of anxiety evaporated. I remembered the previous night, and Paloma, the little village, the old man, and even Vali crossed the stage of my thoughts. Then all was empty.

I'm here. Now. This was the only thought I allowed myself. Tenderly I stroked her thick, dark hair. And without opening her eyes she asked me when I was going off to find the horses.

"*Hola, chica, no lo sé…* I've no idea and I don't even want to think about it at the moment. I'm in another world now."

I could see the tip of a pine tree, framed in the skylight above me, and I watched how the gentle breeze that had come up the hillside played with it. Time passed and hardly seemed to exist anymore. I was here and that was that. Occasionally I nodded off but only for an instant. Strangely enough I seemed to derive pleasure from my feelings of anxiety, perhaps because at the moment these were my only feelings. And then there was Paloma's firm, smooth skin that was lying against me, and I felt her breast pressing against me each time she breathed in. Apart from that I felt nothing.

It was already midday when I got up. Children were playing in the big room below and their cheerful voices echoed through the house. I was as aware of them as I was of the tips of the pine trees in the skylight, and it was almost as if I had witnessed these simple things for the first time in my life. For ages, I stood leaning on a cool projection of the wall, absorbing the sounds. At that moment I was bereft of the willpower or the physical strength to do anything about my future or the horses or the old man.

That evening I was filled with contentment at being among so many agreeable people. I said very little and even when asked a question my answers were brief and to the point. I watched everything that was going on and absorbed it like the mist-saturated air above breaking waves. All the people carried on in a similar fashion—full of energy, wild and bubbly. Men, women, and children were bouncing with life and excitement. I observed it all from the sidelines, but the mist moistened my skin enough to restore my feelings of being alive.

Paloma stayed glued to my shoulder. How was it she understood that I wanted nothing more that encouragement and sympathy? There she was on the very day I needed her, restful and full of strength, even though to look at her I would have thought she appeared unremarkable and soft. With her next to me, I could breathe deeply; although she said and did nothing, in fact she did exactly what was required.

So it was that something inside me began to germinate, though at first it was as intangible as a feeling of sadness when one first wakes. I turned my face toward her and my cheek stirred her hair. Though my breathing was still deep and slow I could catch her fragrant scent just as I could sense her compassion. I asked myself how it was possible that I had never before experienced anything like this.

The next few days produced no change in the situation: day followed night, the sun shone hot again, and I lay resting. Suddenly the weather broke and the warm rain soaked me to the skin. It was Paloma who saw me through this time with her calm strength, only occasionally asking when I was thinking of going to find the horses.

At first I ignored the question; then I said I didn't know.

Finally, I burst out with, "I don't think I shall go. No, I'm staying here a little longer and then I'll return the jeep to the old man. I've changed course. Maybe the old man is right and maybe he's wrong; I don't care a jot but I'm not going to follow the horses."

While I was carrying on like this, Paloma just stared at me, standing silently in a corner of the room. Then she turned and left without a word.

The next day she asked me the same question, and it did not seem to affect her that I answered more irritably than before.

"Why in the world should you concern yourself with this business? I know you have devoted your time to me up here and it's been wonderful, but why should you care what I do? Don't you see you're burdening me with a subject I have already made a thing of the past? It was not easy for me to decide that, but I have and it's finished. Please don't rub salt in the wound."

Once again she stood quietly in the corner of the room, but this time she didn't leave. She came over to me, took my hand, and laid it on her hip. She put her arms around me and for a time we just stood like that until our breathing was to the same rhythm and our bodies seemed to be one. Then I heard myself saying, "Tomorrow morning. Yes, tomorrow morning!"

I was woken by the sound of the jeep door slamming. My first reaction was to be cross and jump out of bed but then I slowly sank back onto the bed. It was still dark outside. *What a woman! What a woman*, I thought. Once again I heard a noise in the room underneath, followed by footsteps and the jeep door slamming again. I didn't react. She'd soon appear and not say a word, I knew.

As on the first day I arrived, all my things were stuffed, ready to leave, into my one old suitcase. Then she did appear and indeed said nothing. I took a deep breath and stayed quite still. I was intensely aware of all the sounds inside and outside the house: footsteps on the stairs, banging doors—and Paloma's gentle breathing, as she approached the bed and sat herself down on the edge, gave me a kiss, and then left.

three

IT IS ALWAYS POSSIBLE to be doing something and have one's thoughts in quite another place. For some days I did what I did without having the sensation of being in any particular place. I wandered about aimlessly, pursuing a tenuous hunch. The dangerous condition of the road fortunately acted as a spur to my consciousness, as I had to pay attention to deal with the wheels getting stuck and the endless slippery loose pebbles. Something inside me continued to worry about the daily grind: the awareness of my actions reached me as if through a mist. I was suffering from hunger and thirst and the pain of it kept me awake. I abandoned the jeep as the road petered out and began following the course of a dry river that I could to some degree negotiate. Paloma had warned me of the danger of scorpions, so I looked carefully in my boots every morning and shook out my clothes.

One night I secured my canvas cover to the undergrowth next to the river, collapsed onto the ground, and ate part of my remaining bread and garlic. My God! How thin I had grown: I was skin and bones. Then I lay down, put my head on my rucksack, and fell asleep.

As I awoke, I remembered in a flash that I had forgotten to make a sketch in my little book of my route on the previous day. I felt a wave of fear when I considered what it would be like to be lost. There was no sign of humans anywhere! I scrabbled about in my rucksack for a pencil and drew the course of the river I had been following. When had I left the river? Ah! I remembered, so no need for panic.

My eyes wandered across the valley, looking for a familiar feature by which I could find my bearings. Then my hands dropped, the sketchbook and pencil falling to the ground. There they were! For heaven's sake, there they were! Across the undergrowth and a wide stony plateau, I counted over twenty horses.

four

"MY GOD! Just look at you now! Come and sit down! Drink this and say if you can eat something! What on earth have you been doing? We've been looking everywhere for you."

"Leave off! It's all right, I'll soon be back on my feet," I said but the words tumbled out with difficulty. "At first things went well, but the return journey nearly did me in. Paloma, I found the horses! I saw them and they saw me. A little water, please! I must start from the beginning—but first some food, Paloma."

It would take time for me to get accustomed to eating proper food again. For days on end I had survived on wild herbs, leaves, and berries. I no longer knew how long it was that I had been away, but it had been more than a month. My stock of food had run out after a short time. Once I had eaten, though, I could begin to put my thoughts in order and recall what I had seen and experienced.

It was the first few days that seemed to be the worst in my memory: I was beset by gnawing hunger so bad that I had to stop for a couple of days, but then I found water and I knew I would be able to exist for some time on what I could gather. There was also enough wood for me to build a fire each evening in order to heat soup that I made from wild leaves and herbs. Thank the Lord I had enough salt.

After a few days Paloma came to me and asked me to tell her about my experiences in the mountains. We sat outside on a wooden bench, looking across open countryside to the distant valley. There was a steep ravine falling away at the perimeter of the village and the birds of prey circled close up to the houses as they took advantage of the rising air. A small round area, protected by rocks, had been left between the houses and the vertiginous drop, protected by carefully laid rocks, and this had for generations been the "village square," where all life took place.

Paloma sat huddled next to me on the bench, dressed only in short trousers made from some fine, thin material. Most people in the village walked about either minimally clothed or completely naked, especially the children. Paloma's skin was dark brown. What a beautiful creature she was!

"I don't know exactly what happened," I began, "but something unique and important for me took place there. How can I describe it? Well, there came a time when I had stopped my search. I could take no more. I had no desire to pass judgment on anything or distinguish between good and bad. All that concerned me was that I was hungry and the fact that I was still alive, but that was not an experience of much importance. I had only seen one or two horses but I had not achieved any real understanding of what was going on with them."

While I was speaking, I was gazing at the pots of flowers on the stone steps of the house opposite and at the long shadows cast by the evening sun. Cheerful children's voices, carried to us on the warm breeze, were the only sounds to disturb the wonderful silence and I listened to them for a time, before continuing.

"When I first caught sight of the horses it was as if I had been struck dumb and I don't know why. It was a little herd of wild horses and I was filled with joy: it was as if, in some way, I had arrived at my destination after a long journey. I was totally exhausted and, strange to say, the pleasure was not that I had found them. It was pure pleasure, nothing more. I tell you this because I am certain that my state of mind was far more important than anything I was doing, or indeed seeing or thinking. My state of mind was the departure point, the journey, and the end point—all in one."

As I was explaining this to Paloma, she sat calmly and without saying a word. Now and again I glanced into her dark eyes. Then I took her hand and tenderly stroked her hair, which draped beguilingly across her shoulders and her breasts. We sat silently next to each other until Paloma looked up and said, "Come on, let's join the others! It's time for dinner. Afterward you can tell me all about it, everything you can remember. Agreed?"

I sprang to my feet, stamped my feet on the rickety boards of the balcony, and shouted as loudly as I could, "*Si, señora — si, señora…!*"

Paloma leaped to her feet and went laughing into the meeting room. I stayed for a while on the balcony because I so loved her uninhibited laughter, to say nothing of the noise of the children yelling and carrying on.

five

AFTER DINNER, I SAT DOWN and told it all to Paloma at last.

"Once I had found the horses, my overriding concern was not to lose them and the thought of doing so caused me a good deal of grief. Suppose I were to frighten them so that they galloped off. How would I ever find them again? As I said, this was my one thought.

"It was only some days later that I realized I would never lose them. I found I had entered into a game, a kind of dance with them that slowly unfolded along the valley, hemmed in by two mountain ranges. At first I kept a careful eye on their tracks, their droppings, the cropped grasses where they had grazed and the flattened areas where they had rested. In fact, in the early days, these signs of their whereabouts were of more interest to me than the horses themselves.

"At first, I only saw the horses from a distance but I was getting to know them by what they left behind. All this while I was very tired and becoming weaker. I had difficulty staying on my feet as I attempted to follow their tracks. I spent the nights where they had rested, although they did not always distinguish between night and day. Usually they rested at night, but occasionally they seemed to be quite lively.

"It was as if one came into a man's house and gradually discovered his habits, his nature, and his characteristics by observing all the traces he left behind. Isn't that a better, more indirect, and at the same time more complex approach than the usual?

"You must understand, I didn't spend my time in deep thought; I let it happen. There was no inner drive urging me on. I wandered along their tracks and even felt they could be doing the same along mine. Then one day even the hunger pangs became bearable: I became accustomed to the lack of food. Living in the mountains and following the horses became more and more of a tangible mode of existence, a sequence of rituals.

"Without really setting out with that intention, I learned about their movements and their habits, even though I was always at a distance from them.

"I had one experience of a very touching nature, although it was so strange I hardly know if it really happened or not. It had been raining when all of a sudden the sun came out. It shone on the bare rocks and the water, glistening on the mountainside, dried in a thin misty film. The mossy inclines were now a dark green but glistened where they caught the light. And how slippery they were when the mist turned the moss into soggy masses! The dust that had settled during the day had been washed down into a sticky layer everywhere, and the last drops of rain were still falling from the branches of the trees. I caught my rucksack against one branch of a knobbly pine; it sprang back and struck my arm a nasty blow that made me turn violently to one side in order to see what it was. It was at that moment that something happened that I still cannot describe accurately. Was he near or far? It all happened in a flash, but the vision of the stallion is still etched in my mind as clearly as when I saw him. He turned abruptly as if shocked and made a leap in my direction, then stood motionless like a shining silver rock—only for a fraction of a second, but for me it was a moment of eternity. Though it happened so quickly, I took in every detail: his gray-brown flanks, his dark eyes, and his fabulous white mane. After that moment's hesitation, he turned away from me and, without glancing in my direction, galloped off into the valley.

"It was only then that I noticed the whole herd had been grazing down in the valley, and I watched as he drove the herd on, his mane flying in the wind. They dashed off through the undergrowth and it was only by observing where the raindrops had been knocked off the vegetation that I was able to follow them. I felt as if I had been struck by lightning.

"You see, Paloma, over many days we had established a mutual agreement about the distance we were from each other that was so subtle and respectful that this incident came like a bombshell. It was only on that one occasion that I saw the stallion so close, but the moment was crucial. That encounter with a properly wild and free creature made an indelible and moving impression on me. It shook me to my core. Yes, I know Vali was wild and mad, dangerous and untamed, but he was at the same time a sad creature. He carried man's suffering on his back; whereas this horse was just himself, his own master. He had not suffered from any distortions caused by contact with human beings; he had not had to adapt to a code of behavior not instinctively his own. His trust in the world he knows is unbroken, and that world is unaffected by human values and ways of life.

"For several days on end I ate practically nothing. My sensibilities were not dulled by modern amenities, not even electric light. I was immersed in the natural world and in a state of total peacefulness. I felt as though I had left the other world behind me, including my old self. I was not even seeking anything; it was almost as if I no longer existed. Suddenly I was confronted with this creature, the incarnation of pure untrammeled life. I felt as if someone were whipping me with a thousand lashes. All the horses I had ever encountered passed in front of me, and not only them but their stalls, the dreary grey riding rings, the trailers, men swearing at the horses and belting them, and the cages they were jammed into on occasion. Likewise, I saw Vali and saw myself making demands on him, pushing him, and coaxing him. Here, by contrast, I could see what it was really like or could be for horses, or perhaps how it was once upon a time, to exist as a shining, proud, elemental force—something I recognized I had been dreaming about for years. Here I was, a little man looking at a real horse."

When I was finished, I sat for a long time, looking down into the valley, without speaking a word. Nor did Paloma disturb the peace with importunate questions. I sat wandering about in my thoughts as if searching for a tune.

"What do you suppose happens, Paloma," I asked, "to someone who unexpectedly has a life-changing experience? Take the example of the man, standing on the threshold of death, who compares his life before some extraordinary experience to that after it. How often do people achieve unexpected fulfillment only because of one event, which could easily have been something they had feared for years, like a serious illness, a setback in their social standing, a divorce, or some other unthinkable blow to their lives? What happens at such moments, and what happened to me in that fraction of a second?"

After a while Paloma replied, "When a body is almost dead, the skin protecting the soul is very thin and therefore surely susceptible to any stimulus that only it can understand and react to. Doesn't that become a permanent influence? Isn't an experience like that an invisible frontier where everything beyond has new values and a new meaning?"

A little later, she continued, "I only wish I could have the experience of believing I would die tomorrow; don't most of us live as though we think we will never die?"

"When I was out there, Paloma," I replied, "I felt in many respects as if I were nearing the end: without food, security, or any living soul nearby. I was in a 'no man's land' between life and death."

"I think I know what you mean," she said. "In fact I know this sort of feeling very well: being the only person capable of action and at the same time being led by the uncertain signs of the time. It's being active and passive in one. You are handed something on a plate but still you try to overstep the boundaries by your own efforts."

I looked into Paloma's eyes and I could see something wholesome and strong. Indeed, I could feel her strength as she went on,

"It's as if one were following oneself and there were no self; as if one were returning by the only road that made sense, that of respect for every living creature. If only the world would do this it would not be destroying itself in the terrible way it is."

six

THE WEATHER BROKE: the nights were cooler and it rained frequently. Autumn announced itself in no uncertain manner. Because the little village was over a thousand meters up, winter began much earlier there than just a few kilometers away to the south, where the mountains met the sea.

Again and again my thoughts traveled back to that empty and despairing landscape where the valley of the horses looked to the west and watched the sun setting between the peaks on either side; to the stream that ran down the valley from the thousand-meter-high mountains behind me, covered in snow. I saw that gently rising, stony landscape with its few large protruding rocks. My mind's eye wandered to those glorious barren meadows that seemed to belong to another world. Whenever I lost the horses and searched for them for days on end, it was there that I had found them. They loved feeding on the long, sour grasses of the water meadows as much as they liked to roll in the sandy mud, which coated them with a layer of protection against the insects and the scorching rays of the sun. It was there that I found them and could once again settle down to watch them intently from a distance. Even my stallion had sometimes appeared to have forgotten his task as he munched the long, tasty green grasses, calmly and as if without a care in the world.

I had hesitated in approaching them more closely for fear they would take fright and leave, but as my love for these creatures deepened, my body was drawn down toward them because I wanted them to be able to see me just as I saw them, and to feel that we shared our secrets.

It was these feelings that led me on and showed me the way even though I hardly understood what I was doing. I soon noticed that the horses in the herd were if anything calmer when they saw me, and when we stood face to face, for now they understood I was making no demands on them. I am certain this is the reason they stood their ground. When in subsequent years I approached horses that were dangerous, horses that had been turned into wild, mad creatures, it was this image that I kept before my eyes and this message that I sent them: *I want nothing from you. I am making no demands.*

When I thought about it later, I saw that this was the key moment, my first real access to the company of horses. It was the foundation of my future work and the first step on my own journey of self-discovery. It became clear to me that this was the only way to success: one has to believe this so completely that one's body demonstrates by all its outer signs the truth *inside*.

How the body demonstrates this so clearly I cannot say, but it does. Any suspicion of something outside this core belief engenders only fear and the desire to flee, and if horses find they cannot flee then the fear is replaced by mistrust and aggression. It is thus that humans must initiate the encounters between themselves and horses.

As I stood close by those wild horses, bursting with life yet peaceable and patient, and acknowledged to myself that nothing in my previous life with horses resonated with what was now happening to me, I already knew that I had made the first and most important step. I had but to recover this state of mind when the relentless hurly-burly of daily life threatened to crush me.

Afterward, I knew one thing for certain: I had found my benchmark. Wherever and whenever I met horses I would recognize immediately from their reaction to me how close or far I was from their true selves thanks to the pitiless introduction that fate had subjected me to during this period. I was right. In the years that followed, although I never had another similar experience, I have never abandoned the trail blazed by that experience.

One day I sat engrossed in my thoughts, and I have no idea how long Paloma sat quietly next to me before I sensed that she was close. I turned toward her and thought how much I owed her.

"As I was standing there, Paloma," I said, "I had my eyes turned to the ground. The stallion had a look at me and then continued grazing. The mares were clustered together and when they moved, the stallion followed suit. It was an example of unity, a group with one mind rather than a collection of individuals. You could not envisage the one without the other: it was not simply a stallion with a bunch of mares and foals. It was a group of horses with a structured, unified form. I went on looking at the ground and then something strange began to take place. I didn't dare lift my eyes up while I made a few steps backward. Listen to what happened then, Paloma! You must try to picture it exactly as it happened. I was apathetic and mentally exhausted. I just stood in a puddle and hardly dared breathe. Only a few paces in front of me stood this vibrant, pure, unspoiled being. And between us there was nothing. Absolutely nothing! And in that instant I knew that I also belonged to that entity, to the herd. In other words, if I should succeed in remaining in the situation in which the herd accepted my presence at relatively close quarters, then I was a part of them and quite simply accepted by the whole body of them.

"Breathing quietly and deeply, I moved almost imperceptibly to one side, at a tangent to the herd. Do you know what happened next? The stallion followed every step of mine precisely. Yes, this wild animal, untamed, who had never had contact with humans, followed every one of my steps. I was a part of the whole and helped to form the whole. I took a step forward; so did the stallion. Do you understand, Paloma? Without a rope or anything connecting us, I was affecting the movements of this wild animal. I don't know exactly how great a distance there was between us: it could have been thirty meters or more, but we were working together. In the end, the mares that led the herd began to move. They formed a circle around the group, while I stood stock still. Then with a loud neighing, the stallion charged toward them and shook his head violently to the right and to the left, and the mares galloped away across the scrub and all followed.

"It was suddenly obvious to me that the understanding between these creatures and myself could only take place when it suited them, with the help of their language—what we call body language—and that had to be exactly right for the moment."

seven

WHAT A STROKE OF GOOD FORTUNE it was during this period to have Paloma at my side. I not only had someone to share the days with but a pleasant companion to help with the daily tasks and duties. Actually, it was more than that: I could not have asked for the company of someone who behaved in a more sympathetic way. Where others would ask endless questions, she would understand, and where others only saw the surface of a problem, she saw beneath it; where others would be impatient and think first of themselves, she was glad to wait and always ready to help. Without having an appreciation of her own strength, she had a kind of innocence that enabled her to concentrate on other people's happiness. Where others might have abandoned themselves to their little idiosyncrasies, she seemed to be part of it, happy to celebrate the successes of others with them but never to be party to any meanness or vulgarity.

In fact, she was what I might call a "real woman." Paloma had not been forced into the inferior role women so often have thrust upon them by men with all their strength. There are plenty of people in the world, but how many of them are ever allowed to become "real men" and "real women"?

During the time I was following the horses, I often thought of Paloma because the experiences I was having seemed to me to fluctuate between opposing extremes. It was similar to the two ends of a bow, held in tension, with the energy stretching along the bowstring representing the two of us and at the same time reflecting what I had witnessed with the herd. With the passage of time I was more and more drawn to this woman whose outward manner was as unremarkable as the strength and true greatness of her inner self was formidable. She succeeded without any embellishment: she was the dancer, always appearing in the most beautiful poses, whether proud and stormy or soft and giving like a delicious sun-kissed fruit.

I asked of the stallion, as I did of her, what power did he represent? Of course, the human being that I saw more and more of was, from the physical point of view, the less powerful of the two: Paloma was slight of build and short, but as the days passed, I saw in her the same beauty that I saw in the stallion. As for her inner strength, it became ever clearer to me that it was even greater than the stallion's. She was the leading force in the village community; she was its soul, and it rested with her alone to decide on the direction the community took.

After I had recovered, I went out to find the horses again sometimes, but I saw nothing more of the stallion in the following weeks. I remained entirely fascinated by the animal as I remembered him, always the leader but never imposing his will with force, let alone violence, and without ever giving a hint of his own strength. He was simply the leader, avoiding any need for confrontation.

In Paloma, I began to feel I had found the key to a better understanding of the stallion and his herd.

eight

ONCE AGAIN SUMMER was upon us and when the clouds thinned, the sun shone with its southern heat on the moist green foliage, filling the air with a richer, stronger variation on the scents of springtime. Indeed, the air was so thick you felt you could grasp it with your hands; it carried all living beings along with it, inviting them to open their hearts, to love, play, forget, laugh, enjoy themselves, and thank God.

One day, Paloma and I were lying behind a little hill, taking shelter after a swim behind some barren plants and letting our skin dry in the mild autumn sunlight—the water in the deep mountain lake was so cold that it was still cooling the soft air around us. We breathed deeply and slowly, allowing our bodies to separate after being thrown together by the shock of the cold water. I felt great and asked Paloma if she felt the same. By that time I had already recovered my usual weight, and thanks to Paloma's company and our untroubled existence, I felt my strength returning.

We had spent the early afternoon working in the garden, digging holes where the autumn vegetables would be stored for use in the winter. There was always plenty of work to do in the village, but as everyone did their best to help, the tasks seemed light. Sometimes as they worked, the villagers sang songs in their dialect, and I too sometimes sang and played on a guitar, though I stopped whenever they sang their songs. The memory of those songs stayed with me for years, and above all, Paloma's quiet, tuneful voice. Indeed, after my departure, when our ways had separated forever, the sound of her voice was my best memory.

But on that sunny afternoon, the winter months still lay ahead of us, and there was nothing to do but enjoy the intimate stillness of the little lake. I found myself using Paloma as a touchstone for my reflections. She, I knew from experience, would help me get to the essentials.

"Paloma," I began, "I'm thinking of one little mare in the herd. What was her secret? What was the basis of her strength and directness? None of the horses, not even the young stallion, left such an impression on me as that mare. Whenever they were grazing, she always stood a little to one side. Although everything you can imagine was going on around her, she let it happen, unlike the other mares who showed much more concern for their young. I also noticed that she stood facing the direction that she would take later when she led the herd onward. Her demeanor was always attentive. Sometimes she looked around at the stallion and occasionally he approached her, but on the whole she remained on her own while the others played among themselves. Without doing anything in particular, she still made her presence felt. If she wandered through the herd she was accepted by all the others and never ever got into a scrap with them, even though two of the other mares, clearly of a lower rank than she, were more muscular, larger, and better looking. She exercised her authority at a suitable distance and when it came time to move on, she circled the herd to gather and prepare them. They all followed her without question.

"What noble creatures they are, and what an extraordinary structure of freedom and oneness holds them together. When they come into contact with human beings who are used to imposing our will with force and cruelty, can you imagine how despicable we are in their eyes? To think that such a weak, undignified creature as a human has the power to subordinate these noble creatures—a proud mare or a proud stallion.

"No, Paloma, there is only one solution and that is to bring these divergent ways of understanding closer together. Humanity will have to establish this sense of dignity that horses recognize and accept in the wild in our own relations with one another. This is the clue that leads us to an understanding of the secrets of the Amazons and the knights of old. They shaped their personalities following the mold of this sense of dignity that really counts in the animal world and allows a proper sense of trust to develop.

"And in our world? Are not the virtues that the lead mare exhibited so wonderfully precisely those we are supposed to value? Is it not the case that these creatures have embodied for millions of years the very virtues man has tried to develop and not properly achieved?"

"So how do you think people should treat their horses?" asked Paloma.

"First of all we have to behave in such a way that the horses understand us. God has given us the power of speech so I can explain things to you by word of mouth. Horses do not have this ability; they have their own way of communicating. I haven't been around horses long enough to have learned it, but now I know it is my duty to devote myself to understanding them. If I can learn to value and respect them, then I shall have made the first step into *their* world, a step nearer to knowing what they are saying. It is the opposite of the usual arrogant wish of humans to bring horses into *our* world, a world of violation, struggle, fury, vanity, and the pursuit of results through ambition and competition. In all the time I was there in the wild, I witnessed none of those qualities. When I look around me at the life of this village, I wonder whether we should not all be going out there to see if we could emulate their lives. It's a question of who should follow the other: should the horses be learning from us or we from them? Surely we should be learning how to achieve what all people long for from them; isn't that the way to understand the message, their message to us?

"I am determined to achieve this. I don't know exactly how, but others, including the old monk, have succeeded in learning from horses what man should do.

"People who want to work with horses first have to learn to acquire the dignity that will allow them to adopt the role of the lead mare. Even the very lowest horse in the pecking order has qualities we must discover and learn to use. Only when we have laid the foundations deep within us will the horse accept and follow us without compulsion or struggle, without the use of a whip or any other means of inflicting pain. The horse will follow us when he can trust in our protection, exactly as he can trust his lead mare in the animal world. Then and only then will the competition riders, show riders, and people intent on winning cups turn into Amazons and knights. Just think of it: if this were to happen, we would have ears to hear, hands to feel, and eyes to see and understand the message of the horses—their message to us."

"And do you believe we would then learn to love, and love genuinely?" asked Paloma.

I had sat bolt upright in my excitement but now I let myself slowly sink back by Paloma's side. How did my heated words stand up to this question, put so gently and briefly?

"You're right, Paloma. Perhaps we will learn to love; perhaps we will understand how to love properly."

nine

WINTER SET IN AT LAST and all the gaps in the buildings were plugged with whatever could be found, but we were still worried that there was not going to be enough firewood for the coming cold months. There was not much to do at that time and everyone withdrew into themselves. If you looked around, you found people sitting about wrapped in thought and composedly waiting for whatever the future held in store.

The weather left me fewer opportunities to go after the horses, but on the occasions I was able to, I still found it an unforgettable experience. I did not dislike my fellow humans but I found refuge in being on my own, so I valued this period of my life. Above all else, I cherished the time spent with Paloma; when we were together we found ourselves speaking almost in whispers as though we were afraid of disturbing our happiness, which lay like a cloak over everything, and the peace of the horses that lived in this boundless landscape. We followed the trails that the horses left in the deep snow and watched them from a distance making their way—not without difficulty—and waiting for spring to return their paradise to them.

For much of the time they did nothing at all and when it snowed they took shelter behind rocky headlands. The snow settled on their coats until they appeared buried in the drifts, part of the white splendor of the mountains. They lived on the sparse vegetation that here and there still found the light of day; they nibbled the bark from trees and sometimes found patches of grass by the banks of the river. It was here by the water that they seemed most contented, playing and frolicking about, especially when the days were clear and the sky turned a deep blue, in contrast with the endless white snow. When the sun, low down in the sky, cast a warm, metallic glaze over the landscape, they raised their heads high in the air and their nostrils quivered; the foals beat the snow with their legs and chased each other, while the adults groomed their thick winter coats. They used this time to recuperate and it was as if they were refueling, breathing in the warmth of the sun to store it against the cold nights and make them more bearable.

Then a fresh snowfall would cover their hard-won tracks and once again it was the lead mare that walked at the front of the line to beat a path, using her lowered head as a snowplow to make it easier for the others. She literally shoveled her way up the mountainside, using her hind legs for purchase on sloping or icy patches and seldom pausing for rest. One sensed the ravages of the winter months and of the extra effort expended in being the leader, even though her body was concealed under a thick coat. Small wonder that my admiration for her grew with each encounter!

It was on one of those winter days that Paloma and I were at a point in the eastern part of the area where two springs cascade out of the rock face side by side. The water had gouged out a giant chair, wide enough for the two of us to sit. There we were, pressed against each other, looking out over the whole valley toward where the sun sets when we saw the herd to our left and Paloma spoke.

"Did you know the word 'chief' in some Native American languages also means 'the one who serves'?"

This was all she said and for the rest of the time we sat looking at the horses in the valley.

When we returned to the village that evening I began the task of putting my thoughts in order and forming the outline of the book I planned to write about my experiences. This is what I wrote:

The principle of leadership: When people wish to lead others and to do so in a natural and proper way, they have to do it in the manner of these creatures, without the use of power and oppression, so that those who follow agree to be led entirely of their own free will. So it is that the one who is answerable for the group is not the one who has fought for it but the one who has earned it. Nature chooses the one to lead who serves all the others.

Therefore, my first principle for working with horses is that everything I do must be for and in the sole interests of the animal. This will be my first and most important principle of nature.

During the coldest months that came upon us, I buried myself in a corner of the room and filled my notebook with short sentences. I thought for long periods and walked about in that little room with its white walls and peeling plaster before continuing to write.

I may have discovered and understood the principles involved in leading horses, but these rules extend to all parts of the human psyche. We have to awaken the enthusiasms that lie at the foundation of human behavior and learn to go with nature and not against it—it is the duty of everyone that has anything to do with horses to work in this way. So, for a start, we must study the nature of the horse. For how can one possibly work with a horse in the way that suits his nature if we don't know anything about him?

I remembered my first riding lesson, seated, under a cold neon light, on a mare I knew nothing about except for her name. I wrote about her desire for freedom being her most powerful thought and that I, as a man, should never rob her of this. I wrote about the reins and how they should only have a symbolic function, and about the spirit of the horse that lies at the heart of all the beauty of her movements. I wrote about the sense of balance and distribution of the rider's weight and how the horse's equilibrium must never be interfered with in the course of any action. Then I thought of that first riding lesson again, and of all the other people who were going endlessly around and around, around and around, their stiff and awkward bodies being dragged along as though they were dead.

I wrote about the urge that horses have to learn, about the sense of playfulness even among the oldest mares—about their alertness and unfailing inquisitiveness, their sensuality and sense of achievement; and then I thought again of horses I had known and the unnatural way in which they were kept in a state of boredom in stalls and in tiny desolate paddocks, and the way people worked them. I wrote of their yearning to live a free life, without fear, and then my mind turned to the world I came from, the world of dressage in which the aid of choice is so often that of punishment, fear, and anger. And so finally I wrote in large letters my basic principle that would be the most important element in my future work:

If you go against the principles of nature, you go against the very essence of a being. If you go against this essence you will surely build resistance.

The resistance will be against the person who caused it. This sort of resistance is commonly met with more violence, which only serves to create stronger resistance. In other words, it is a vicious circle that only has two possible outcomes.

One ends in the person being badly hurt, because aggression responds to violence by becoming stronger—and, most probably, also in the death of the horse in the slaughterhouse.

The second possible outcome of this spiral is the pathetic resignation of the horse, who simply gives up the struggle, withdraws into himself, and obeys without any joy or spark in the eye—a spark that can be recognized in the wild horses from a hundred yards away—and endures a kind of slavery to the end of his life.

How was I to find the way, I asked myself, to those people who had adopted another method of working with horses? Where was the road?

I wrote: *One has to work day in and day out to absorb those qualities that horses possess. How can you be worthy of another creature when you are bound hand and foot in a world lacking in dignity? How can you care for the freedom of another creature when you yourself are a prisoner?*

One must be sure to record every battle because even if you should win one, you lost it the moment you engaged—participating in battle at all is a sign of weakness because it is to do with wielding power and aggression.

Find your own internal equilibrium, both physical and mental; how can you ever expect to maintain the fine balance of a horse if you are out of kilter? Appreciate that life is always an open book so you must always be eager to learn. If you only know how to grow more and more rigid in your ideas, how can you begin to understand the horse's desires?

Search for the reason in everything you do and act only when you understand what that reason is, not because someone tells you to do something or because it is routine. If you act without understanding the reasons for your actions, how will you ever understand the reasons for the actions of another creature?

The days and the weeks followed one another as I recorded my thoughts. When spring arrived, people were supposed to be coming to lift some young stallions and mares from the herd. It would be a new beginning like the germination of seeds, the blooming of the spring flowers, and the rain. I realized it was also time for me to have a new beginning. It was time for me to pack my bag and return to the old man and my horse.

During that period there was a horse disease spreading through Spain, and when I returned years later to see if I could find my wild mare and my wild stallion, I found only the valley with the two springs and the seat hewn out of the rock. All signs of the horses had disappeared and even when I went to the spot where I always knew I would find evidence of them, there was nothing.

A farm worker I met later told me that when the pestilence came to that area, the horses were confined to stalls. The pestilence passed but the man thought the stallion had not survived and had been put down in the end by a vet. I thanked the man for the information. When I reached the young people's village, it too was abandoned. I sat down on the balcony and thought of Paloma and of the winter I had passed with her and the children. I remembered my departure and how I said goodbye to her. I would have loved to have seen her again, and I recalled how sad I was when I got into the jeep to return to the old man.

But on the day of my departure, I did not know any of this. A song I knew the lyrics to was playing on the radio, so I sang along with it. As I sang louder and louder, I felt a certain pleasure at the prospect of seeing the old man and I could hardly wait to see my Vali again. I wanted to meet him in the same way I had met the stallion who had helped me to find my way and to whom I felt so grateful.

PART V

··

They Called It
"The Other World"

one

TOWARD NOON ON THE FOLLOWING DAY I reached the old monk's house. I drove slowly up the steep, narrow road and glanced toward the white stallion. I felt a catch in my throat as I thought of the months I had spent there. Then suddenly, there he was, as if he had been expecting me, standing in the shadow of the roof. Before I could greet him, he said, "You've been away a long time."

I took a deep breath before replying, *"Hola—como estas?"* and I thought I detected a small sign of pleasure in his features.

"You are right. I *have* been away a long time—I didn't want to come before I felt the real desire to do so."

My eyes wandered across the house, the garden and the surrounding landscape and I wondered if everything had changed or whether it was I who was observing it all with different eyes. Finally I turned back to the monk and asked him, "How is Vali?"

He hesitated for a moment before replying, "Well, how do you think he is? I don't think he's missed you. Not long ago, I took him back under my care as I thought you would be coming one of these days."

I settled myself in the moss-covered hollow in front of the house, where the cats usually lounged about in the sun and gazed into the valley below. The old man asked me in a friendly way whether I wanted something to eat but I said, "No, but thank you! If it suits you, I would like to go and see Vali."

Vali was in the yard in front of the shepherd's house and I noticed that a part of the fence was new. The yard that had previously been a rectangle was now a full ten-meter-by-ten-meter square. In a far corner, Vali stood dozing. It was a spot sheltered from the wind by a cliff to the west, and it also caught the warmth of the morning sun.

When he noticed my arrival he stood stock still. He was the same distance from me as I had often been from the wild horses; in fact, I never came nearer than this. I suppressed the urge to go up to him, maybe disturb him, and to stroke him. I knew that if I took a couple more paces toward him, he would certainly lay back his ears, bare his teeth and lunge at me so, for a long time, I stood quietly watching him and thought, No, *no one can take away from me what I experienced with those wild horses.*

After a while I asked the old man if he had worked Vali at all. Standing only a few meters behind me he answered in a quiet voice.

"No, he's your horse."

Yes, he is my horse, I thought—and how often had I rehearsed this moment in my thoughts, the moment when for the first time I would meet him after my long absence? The sensation I had deep in my belly was like waves on calm water when someone throws a stone. What else could I do but accept the situation as it was?

I knew it was my body that had to react, not my brain and my understanding. I felt it all deep down just as the old man must have. Everything is there: one has to have the will to let it emerge and declare itself. As long as I allowed fear to be paramount, as long as I had the desire to act and not let things take their course, as long as I had the urge to engage with him rather than accept him, I knew I would never change my horse's attitude toward me.

Body and soul can work together—the one can accept and love, the other can simply be and follow its instincts. I felt strong and powerful and I had the sensation of a strongly pulsating life force inside me.

By forgetting limitations and not dwelling on obstacles, it is possible to happen upon moments of total unexpectedness, a sudden desire to try something new and unheard of. You break out of the confines of your limitations; you are changed and free to act. It's as if you were allowed a peek into a magnificent room in a king's palace that had so far been forbidden territory for you. Once seen, the memory stays, even when life returns to its accustomed tenor. It dances before your eyes like a glowing light and, henceforth, shows you the way you must take. What was about to happen with my horse was an experience like this and stretched beyond the limits of any experience I had so far come across. Achieving the same success with other horses would take years of study, mistakes, failures, and the smallest imaginable step-by-step progress.

When I saw how Vali was standing in the corner of the yard I felt glad to see him again. Whatever might happen, I thought, it will be good. I dared move a little closer to the fence, where I remained, standing calmly and reminding myself to pay attention to how I was holding myself and moving, and how I used my body. Quite suddenly I was aware of a strange feeling: I felt I trusted Vali and was able to devote myself to him. The last thing I wanted to do was to spoil the moment. I moved with a light step and was totally relaxed.

But now Vali made an aggressive move in my direction. He galloped toward me in a wide arc with his head held sideways and upward as he bared his teeth. I was shocked but my breathing remained calm and even, and my body motionless and relaxed. I don't know why but I was suddenly quite certain that he would not bite me and would not have done so even had I been on his side of the fence. Were not all his attacks on me merely the expression of his deep-rooted fear of me as a person?

I'm not going to ruin this opportunity, I kept on saying to myself, not out of fear or out of weakness. I felt no anger toward him. I was even smiling at him. I twisted around all of a sudden and launched myself toward his hindquarters. I did this so swiftly and with such energy that it had the effect of turning him around so that he was facing me. For a fraction of a second I was amazed at this reaction, but I averted my gaze from him in order to show him that I was not asking for anything, no more than I had from the wild horses.

"I'm not asking you for anything, Vali," I said in a voice so gentle that it was little more than a thought. I stared at the ground in front of his feet, remained in a relaxed state, and felt almost the same as I had in the wilderness with the wild horses. I took a step backward and thought, *He's never looked at me as he is at this moment.* I sensed my body telling me what I should do. The situation was similar to what I had experienced in the river valley so I took another small step backward and although my eyes were trained on the ground I made sure I could see what Vali was doing.

I still felt no trace of anger even though he laid his ears back again. I leapt over the wooden fence to the other side and looked directly at him. I remained still and had the overwhelming feeling that he was not going to attack me, to a degree that I had never had before.

Vali. Don't do it! Don't attack me!

As my feet for the second time banged on the hard ground, he swung his hindquarters violently in the other direction and looked at me again, but this time his gaze was noticeably softer and I noticed that he was moving his lower lip. He looked to the right and my body moved fractionally to the left. It was precisely the same game I had played with the wild stallion and Vali's reaction was also the same. Again I stared at the ground, took a deep breath, and moved close to the fence. Vali put his ears back for a moment and then pushed his nose forward and sniffed my hand. I gently stroked his nostrils and played with his soft lips.

I had been able to do this sort of thing when he was ill but never since. I felt how tenderly he pushed my hand and how his soft tongue licked the salty sweat from my fingers. I also had the impression that his eyes were larger than they had been—they were now the playful eyes of a young pony. It was as if, for the first time, his true nature had broken through a crust of fear and panic and come to the light, as if a little piece of his original, undamaged being had revealed itself.

In the end, I turned quietly to the old man and asked him to fetch me a rope. He brought it to me without saying a word and I knew this was the moment to approach Vali.

At first, he laid back his ears and galloped away. I took care to move quickly to the side and stood still, keeping an eye out for his hindquarters. He stopped and turned sideways to me, but instead of running away as I had always done before, I sprang toward him with such determination that I was able to put my arms around his neck and bring him to a stop. Vali stood as if rooted to the ground. He stood there, I didn't move a muscle, and he stared at me.

Very quietly and gently, I said to him, "*Hola, Vali—caballo mio—hombre—como estas?*" "Hello, Vali—my horse—buddy—how are you?"

Slowly he turned his head, looked toward his stall, then back at me, looked toward his stall again and then once more at me.

Suddenly he jutted his lower jaw forward, and stretched out his neck and his head in such a manner that I saw the whites of his eyes underneath the black pupils. He stretched out with all his weight on the front legs and allowed his head to sink down, before snorting several times loudly. I had the feeling this was the first time in his life that he had unwound in front of a human being. Suddenly he appeared soft and biddable as if he had recovered something beautiful from a previous existence. Indeed, he was now quiet, happy, and relaxed, so I made a move toward him. In the same instant, he made a move in my direction and walked slowly toward me until he was close by my side. He was sniffing me everywhere and uttering little snorts while I placed my hand softly on his neck and it seemed to me that a gentle, blameless creature had emerged from a thick, tough shell back into life. The whole bearing and look of the horse had changed—he felt good to the touch and his coat shone with life. As the flat of my hand inched its way around his body he simply gazed into the valley below. As I made to leave him he followed me with a lowered head, exactly as the wild horses had followed the little lean mare.

The old man had never taken his eyes off us but at that point he said to me, "You still have lots to learn—yes, lots."

I myself was still not aware of the full significance of my experience with this horse regarding my future, but the old man knew. He understood, though he never put it into words, that it was not I who had changed Vali, but rather the horse and the whole experience that had changed me.

It was like the transformation of a witch into the prettiest princess, all because a weedy, immature young man who had never learned to doubt the good in the world gave her a kiss and released her from an enchantment. This naïve youth was prepared to believe that through the power of a simple kiss, a wonderful creature would be able to liberate herself from the hideous exterior she was hidden beneath. And this spell, once lifted, also held a promise to free the youth to become king—all by kissing the witch. So, when the enchantment broke, the princess became herself, as she had been all along, her true self no longer concealed; it was the naïve youth who was transformed into something he had never been before. (No doubt the youth stole many kisses thereafter and grew into a fine man.)

two

THE MONK AND I sat together that evening and even though the inner surfaces of the living room walls were warm with the day's sun, a little fire burned in the hearth. Our dinner consisted of bread, garlic, oil, cheese, and tomatoes, washed down with wine. By now the old man felt more like an old friend and I no longer had the feeling that I was disturbing his peace. I felt more like a guest he was taking trouble to entertain.

Because of this I didn't embark immediately on the story of my experiences. It was only after a while that he asked me if I had found the stallion and the herd, and then I told him all about what had happened. He listened attentively without reacting and then asked if I had found the seat so nicely carved out of the rock face and whether I had sat on it.

Of course, I said, I had indeed sat on it and he asked whether I had noticed anything. I told him that at first I was always too exhausted to notice anything, but then I became aware I always felt better for doing so and subsequently took the opportunity of sitting there whenever I could.

"But how on earth do you know about all that?" I asked. "Surely you had no idea where the horses were?"

"I didn't say I had no idea where the horses could be found. I indicated an area where you would find them—more, I didn't say, but, believe me, I know where they are at any time. People will tell you all sorts of stories about the horses but I know almost everything there is to know about them."

I pushed my chair back against the wall and said in a low voice, "I want to thank you for everything you have done for me, but tell me, please, when I should be on my way from here. I would love to stay and develop what began with Vali today. It was perhaps only a small step but for me it was beyond all my expectations. He followed me with a lowered head and was filled with a spirit of freedom. I could not have wished for more."

"Yes, indeed, he showed you his sense of freedom for the first time, that tremendous sense that all horses have. It was the result of your not asking for anything, just being, even if only for a fleeting moment."

He looked thoughtfully but contentedly at the fire before continuing, "You are a witness to what goes on in people's heads. You are the mirror for the humiliation, the cruelty, the lies, and the vanity of humankind but also of the seeds of truth."

I lay back and closed my eyes, listening to the crackling of the fire and I thought how easy life could be. As a rule, I wondered, what does it mean when we say, "I love you"? Does it not in fact signify, "I want you to love me," or "I want to own you," or "I want you to drive away my loneliness," or "I will achieve security when I am certain of possessing you"?

It is only when we find the strength in ourselves to live and to be what we are that we have the right to go to other beings, whether human or animal, and while leaving them as we find them say, "I love you and I want nothing from you."

To be devoted without asking for devotion in return, to be friendly without demanding friendship, because we are self-sufficient and we no longer need the other individual to assure our security or combat our loneliness—that is when the other individual can give us trust and closeness, and we can accept it as a token of pure happiness, without any fear that what we have will be taken away from us.

I thought about Vali also, and how our encounter was so totally different from before. With his unyielding character, he had rejected people over the years and as a result suffered violence and punishment. Every single act of violence would have elicited the same thought from Vali: "Be aware of what you are doing, of who you are and how you act and to whom you are doing violence! Can you not see the suffering in my eyes? Have you noticed the creases on my forehead? It's easy for you to condemn me, to humiliate me, to strike me, in sum to do to me whatever you want because I only stand in the corner and make no sound. I shall store up all the beatings, the tears, and the pain until I give up the ghost. If only you would stop thinking of yourself and your wishes for one instant and think of what I want, I who am another living being no different from you and could present you with a valuable gift if you would only allow it—namely, yourself!"

three

THE OLD MONK'S CLASSES were now a regular event. He corrected me and paid particular attention to my body position. Time and time again he referred back to Vali and my history with him.

"The two of you are building something new, something that was born when you first met but which fell apart when you separated. Between those two events, something was created that has brought you together, a place where the trust and truth between you abides."

The next day I succeeded in resting my hand on Vali's back.

"Don't think about what you are doing," said the old man, "because if you do, you will frighten him again. Live for the moment; be self-contained. There's the horse, his back, and your hand. The most important element connecting these is the trust between you both. When you feel it, you destroy his fear; when you destroy his fear you also destroy his memories, and when you wipe out his memories he can really see what sort of man you are."

For a long time I stood next to my horse and heard the old man making approving noises.

"Stand beside your horse, put on his saddle-cloth, and don't leave him for a second!"

The old man brought me the saddle-cloth and I spread it on Vali's back, disturbing him as little as possible. Then the old man brought the saddle and I placed it in position.

It was thus that I recognized more and more of my own qualities in Vali. I could see reflected in his nature my absentmindedness as well as my depths; my superficiality as well as my earnestness; my surface fears as well as my warm, sympathetic, and open self. In spite of his advanced years, the horse blossomed as the weeks passed: his eyes became brighter, his coat shone, his step was more elevated and he looked prouder of himself. In the end, he let me climb onto the saddle.

"Be watchful," said the old man, "and be aware of everything to do with the horse. Feel the earth under you through his body. Exercise him as he exercises you. If you stop being conscious of him he will feel alone and behave as such. Everything will fall apart. It's only when you maintain the connection with him and feel the earth underneath—every stone, the dusty ground, the soft moss—in the same way that the horse feels these things that he will see the world through your eyes. His wishes will be yours and his actions will be the fruit of those wishes you gave up on some time ago."

Vali and I turned left and right and varied the tempo, and when I brought him to a halt, my breathing was even and regular and I was simply living in the moment. The old man stood there in the sunlight without saying a word until I noticed that his shadow had disappeared and I was alone with my horse. All thought ceased and it was as if I felt the stones under me and the soft mosses.

Finally the day arrived when we both saddled our horses and set off, the old man leading. Without having to make any decisions, I just enjoyed myself. Yes, I do not hesitate to admit it, even though the old man scolded me when he read the unrestrained joy on my face and the boundless pride. This first ride through the mountains was like a triumphal procession and everything seemed to rejoice: the trees and shrubs that peppered our route, the wildflowers, and the sunlight. Somehow, I rose above the old man's severe demeanor, though it wasn't long before that too changed and he was laughing with me. Once again I felt the stones and the mosses and listened to Vali's breathing. I stroked his soft coat and knew that the desperation I had endured for so many months was now obliterated: I was living in this world on the back of this horse.

four

EVERYTHING HAS AN END and it was time for this memorable part of my life, comprising so much sadness and so much happiness, to come to a close. My days spent with the old man were full of nostalgia for me because it made a tie between us that I had never known to exist in this form. Perhaps for the very reason that our trust in each other had grown over the months, the old man decided to give me one more piece of advice: I should gather all my experiences with him, with Paloma in the village, and with the wild horses, and interpret them in my own fashion.

I remember clearly how we got into the jeep before sunrise, taking provisions and having previously arranged with a farmer in the valley to look after our horses, headed off through the village on the national highway. It was a beautiful, clear morning. The old jeep roared along the nearly deserted road but we had hardly begun to speed up after leaving the mountains when the road began another twisting ascent. In front of us, a half-circle of mountains reared up as if to touch the sky: they were an odd gray color veined with strange lines. At their base was a sparse strip of greenery and to the left a narrow rock face with a noticeable bulge in the middle. By this time the morning sun was already hot, indeed much too hot for the time of year. It was not long before even the air blowing over us as we drove along was insufficient to keep us cool. I felt thirsty and lacking in energy.

When I asked the old man where we were going, he made no reply. At the end of the rock face I saw in the distance a three-cornered breach in the wall as if it had been made on purpose. After a few kilometers we passed through the gap and followed a narrow road through a strange landscape that led finally to a monastery. We entered through simple outbuildings and found ourselves standing under the merciless sun in an inner court—the first hint of the splendor that was hiding behind the unprepossessing walls. The small windows of the monks' quarters, concealed behind dark shutters, watched over the eerily empty space as our footsteps rang out in the stillness.

The old man said a few words to me in an almost reverent voice: "Only very seldom are people granted entry to this place, an entry that quite possibly shows them the way to a new dimension. Whether the opportunity is taken depends entirely on the willpower, the strength, and the alertness of the person seeking help."

In spite of the air of peacefulness all around us, I was by now in a state of high excitement; never before had the old man emphasized an event in this way. *It must be something very special*, I thought to myself.

He went on, "Just as the destiny of an individual becomes mired in increasingly complex cycles, so do the inner workings of all humanity. And just as there are extraordinary moments that stand out in the destiny of an individual, similarly there are milestones in the destiny of the human race. This is one such milestone. My object in introducing you to this place is not to turn back the wheel of time but to awaken in you the consciousness of that great trail that joins one important age to the next."

As we walked slowly across the inner court, the old man said in a voice that was so hushed that it hardly seemed intended for my ears, "You see, humanity is but a drop of water in a mighty river—we don't only live for ourselves."

We turned to our left, mounted a short staircase bordered by a fine, curved stone parapet that led into a narrow passageway. It smelled strange: candles in cast-iron holders were burning between small niches in the walls, each containing a stone carving. Below them was an inscription that I was unable to make out. We arrived at a stone portal: a monk sat to one side of it, as if he were expecting us. He rose to his feet, bowed to the old man, and opened a massive iron-decorated door. Down a few steps, we found ourselves in a great hall.

"Until this day," said the old man with pride, "no one like you has been in this place."

A massive table almost filled the space; we were led down one side of the hall and began a tour through a maze of rooms and passageways. I have no memory of how long it lasted, but eventually we entered a number of rooms where gravestones were laid out at regular intervals, decorated with the strangest faces and always including the equal-sided cross of the Templars. The shapes and the figures were fascinating: the finely interwoven patterns combined ornamentation, symbolic shapes, heads, limbs, bodies, and wings with a strangely gentle and peaceful effect. Everything was imbued with secret signs and strange detail: here, a prickly body arranged in a perfect circle; there, unnumbered pairs of eyes. My attention was drawn to a small bas-relief of a horse with a human head; the gaping mouth, the tail, and the wild hair were full of menace.

The old man remarked, "What you are looking at represents many events, in particular the rebirth of humanity."

Before I could ask him what he meant by these strange words, he continued, "At present you do not understand anything of what you are looking at, but soon you will be able to read these symbols like a book."

In the meantime, I let everything drift past: the Templars' signs and arms, marble panels engraved with script, swords and pictures of horses, and more and more gravestones placed on the floor. When I trod on them, they made a dull sound and moved a little. I passed depictions of lions and birds of prey intertwined and seemingly swallowing each other, and the Roman wolf, nursing her twin boys and foaming at the mouth as she stared into the pale faces of the church dignitaries. I found knives and swords, bows and arrows, faces making wild grimaces with tongues jutting out, as well as many images that appeared to be from cultures unknown to me. Protruding from an altar were strange cubes and bullet-shaped objects. The more I saw, the smaller and less confident I felt.

I looked up at the magnificent arched ceiling, which was covered with golden stars twinkling on a deep blue firmament. I looked at the flags contained in glass cases and knew that I had quite lost my bearings. As if out of nowhere, eerie beings began to appear and change and retreat.

Finally the old man led me into a kind of chapel, circular in form—even the benches were curved. There were no windows to bring any daylight into the interior. He sat me down on a bench and settled himself next to me.

"Now, sit quietly and listen to what I have to tell you!"

I leaned against the wooden back and felt overcome by a feeling of deep inner calm. When the old monk began to speak his voice seemed unnaturally deep and distant.

"You seek the message of the horses—*their* truth? You are so close to receiving it, though you keep on straying away from it. However, I know that you really are searching for it and because of this I have brought you here so this unconditional approach in your nature doesn't wreck everything."

I looked at him questioningly, but he went on as if he had not noticed me.

"The secret is to leave things be and start always from scratch as though it were the first day of your life."

"Yes," I answered uneasily.

"You are still looking at the world and horses with the eyes of someone who has not set aside the rigid pattern of his past. Of course these creatures can be described by their outlines, by their appearance, but in truth none of that exists. As long as people are not begging for virtuous qualities, dignity, and morals, they are not seeking to change the old framework. They are only attaching themselves to a new framework with the same insistence that attached them to the old."

I failed to understand what he was getting at, so he asked me to follow him. We went out of the curved double doors through which we had entered and followed a vaulted passageway branching off to the right. We soon reached a space with two benches facing each other. Over the left bench was a small opening through which a little sunlight and fresh air reached the poorly lit passageway. I only paused for a moment at this spot to catch a glimpse of the cloudless blue sky, but when I turned around the old man was no longer there. I was overcome by a not-very-good feeling, but in spite of having the urge to look for him, something inside me held me back. I continued hesitatingly down a passageway that grew ever darker and narrower.

"So you did follow me!"

I gave a start—I had not noticed the old man standing in the recess of a door just next to me. He opened the door, which was plain and heavy and lacked adornment, in sharp contrast to everything else we had seen, and we found ourselves in an irregular, almost oval room. A simple bench stood along the far wall and to both sides of it candles were hanging against the bare stone walls. The walls seemed to be dark brown or almost black so that I could hardly make out anything in the gloom. The far end of the room disappeared into a curved passage. A few small candles that appeared to have been lit only moments ago stood about on the floor. When my eyes had become accustomed to the gloom I could make out a vaulted room filled with shadows cast by the flickering candles. I could see that it was crammed with countless objects like bas-reliefs and other ornaments.

We sat down on the wooden bench. I felt paralyzed and said nothing. Both the darkness and the shape of the room had the effect of concentrating my gaze on the objects so that I gradually lost any idea of the size and shape of the room. The flickering lights gave me the illusion that the walls themselves were moving about and the objects seemed to break loose and swim in a pulsating flow.

"What do you see?" asked the old man. I hesitated before replying so he repeated sternly, "I'm asking you, what do you see? Tell me straight away what you can see!"

"Everything—all the objects seem to be swimming around before us," I replied.

"What objects can you see? Describe their shapes to me! Describe everything you think you can see!"

Once again, his voice had a note of severity that made me frightened to describe what I thought I could see. The light cast by the dark red candles appeared to transform a part of the vaulted room into a pale green color. I sought to understand this phenomenon by searching my previous experience and while I was thinking about this, the green color began to fade and everything looked once again as it had when we entered. At that point the old man told me to get up and take a couple of steps forward. I rose to my feet and stepped into the space in front of me.

"That's far enough! Stand still and look to your front," he told me. "Describe everything you can see now."

The green colors were much paler than before and the objects had lost any recognizable shape. By this time I felt quite ill: my cheeks were drawn inward and my mouth was dry, my tongue hot, and my hands sweating. I begged him to desist, but he hissed at me, "No, not yet! Tell me if you see something that you recognize and can put a name to!"

I felt as though something invisible were attacking the pit of my stomach and about to faint with fear when I noticed that the objects in the room were transforming into faces and masks with horrible grimaces. What had appeared to be dark spots became staring eyes with flame-red pupils; what had looked like serrated lines became hideous teeth, seen through a poisonous green veil and shrouded in a dull orange light. My eyes were playing tricks to such an extent that I no longer knew the stone-built room we had entered; as if I had lost myself in a ludicrous dream, I began to stammer words a helpless child might use when torn away from a usual feeling of safety and overcome by fear and cold. I felt a pressure in my skull that began deep down at the back and then grew in intensity and sharpness. The more I tried to concentrate on what I could make out in front of me, the worse the pain behind my eyes and in my forehead became. Instinctively I put my fingers to my eyes, but the slightest touch only aggravated the pain. I had never in my life felt such pain in my head: it seemed to be gouging out my eyeballs.

In the end I staggered backward and leaned against the doorpost, with my hands in front of my face. What in God's name had I seen? What power could have been responsible for it? The old man led me back into the passageway, where I caught a glimpse of the sun shining through a small opening in the wall.

We each sat on one of the benches and I could see that the old man's expression was friendly again. Indeed, he seemed to be amused at my predicament.

"What on earth was that?" I asked in a whisper.

"That was you," he replied.

five

SLOWLY A FEELING OF CALM returned to my body but I could not yet begin to understand what had taken place. I don't know why, but my mind wandered back to the wild stallion and to Paloma, and I heard the children's voices in the village echoing in the narrow alleyways. I saw the bright strips of sunlight, already growing weaker with the setting sun, as they moved across the walls of the vaulted room. We must have sat in silence for some time before the old man began to speak again.

"Your questions, doubts, and fears still show clearly in your features. When will you realize that every support you grasp at is a crutch? Whenever you lose it, you risk falling over. Why do you still rely on it? You are standing before the door: push it open! Pluck the fruit: the horses have shown you where to find it; they have shown you so much. If only you could trust yourself and them a little more. You squirm about like a prisoner who chastises his liberators because they want to rob him of his chains."

"But it takes time," I murmured.

"You are right. It takes time."

I was gradually becoming calmer and my consciousness returning to the here and now. "Please explain to me what took place just now. What was it that I saw and felt and what has it all to do with my quest and its secrets? What is the connection with the message of the horses?"

The old monk leaned toward me and I thought I detected signs of a certain pleased anticipation.

"Look at my hand," he said, holding up the palm of his left hand under my eyes. "That's the hand of an old man. There's skin, cells, bones, and veins carrying blood. But is that the whole story? Look at what it tells you about me, what it has to say! Does not my hand tell you about me, just as yours tell us about you? What sort of language is it using to tell us these things? It is the language of uncertainty, the language of feeling. It is what the wild horses and the uncompromising quality of nature taught you. This language is a door into another world. What you have learned is only a splinter from another larger dimension. Another reality floats over this hand made of flesh and blood. And which of these two realities is most important for our existence and our lives? Is it important that at this point a blood vessel disappears and that the inner surface of the skin is a paler shade than the outer? Or is it more important that this hand speaks of goodness, of giving and loving, and that another hand might reveal a history of destruction, grasping, and grief? Which is more important:

that we see or that we do not see the things we sense in another way? The language of so-called reality or the language of the spirit?"

The old man leaned back at this juncture and I noticed how the strips of sunlight had moved up and to the right, becoming less defined as they turned to a gentle red and covered the old gray walls. I felt my strength returning as the uncertainty and fear retreated with the same speed with which they had attacked me.

I noticed a gentle smile on the old man's face and I was aware that my features were also softening. I was on the way to my goal and I didn't want to worry about when and where. Nothing would now put me off.

Whatever was to come, I wanted to be in the driver's seat.

"Tell me, were all those things I saw an illusion? All the colors and shapes: were they merely my mind's inventions?"

"I would rather call it a little game. It was no more than that, but enough to put us both on the right track. You needed to be impressed with the absurdity of the idea that there is one entrenched reality, which of course there isn't. What your eyes showed you were shapes arranged and produced in such a manner that your imagination and your unconscious mind had plenty of room for interpretation. It was not *a* reality, but it was *your* reality. At the moment you saw those objects and shapes, you were witnessing your own experiences and feelings. Truth is what your mind at any particular moment interprets from the visible and invisible aspects of what you see. Your innermost self paints a picture, a 'truth,' which you then believe exists. If you achieve awareness of what you have seen, you are conscious of the inner and outer elements combining, of the way in which the frontiers begin to melt. What you took for inviolable truth melts like a pat of butter in the sun. If you continue further along this path then a new world opens before you."

"Then why did these images produce such a reaction of horror in me?" I asked him.

"Because one of the worlds I describe cannot exist without the other. The sun gives us life, warms us, and lights our way by day, but it is also a destroyer: it causes drought, creates deserts, and causes catastrophes. There is no such thing as life without death. The moon shines with its cold light, the sun radiates heat. There is good fortune and misfortune."

I detected in the old man's features a glow of enthusiasm, a quiet happiness that I had previously noticed whenever he was in the company of his horse. He was always encouraging his white stallion to find his own way and to mature wisely. At that moment, I had the feeling that his attention was concentrated on me in the same way.

"Forget about the pictures—or think of them as just a part of you, things you carry with you that develop and change. Perhaps during their short life they will trigger something in you, another step on the road to discovering other important secrets of horses. Consider their brief existence as a part of the lesson we receive, showing us that there is another world apart from the one we think we see. For our forebears, the Celts, and those who have followed in their foot-steps, this lesson is an inescapable fact. We know they referred to this other world as simply that: 'the other world.' It was a world that our modern rules of logic could live without and therefore ignored: the spiritual, emotional world. It was their holy world."

Now it was only the tiny candle flame that illuminated the

passageway with flickering, tender light. The intermittent sound of the wind had also died away and I could sense the splendor and the power of these ancient walls.

"Living with horses is a constant act of mastering oneself. Given that you are someone who seeks the truth, the existence of a horse next to you requires your unfailing good will and your humility as long as the horse is alive."

The old man stood up and indicated that I should follow him. We retraced our steps without hurrying and, as if not wanting to disturb the stillness of the evening, he spoke in a whisper to me.

"Our forebears did not look for the meaning of life in the material world. They sought to abandon the rigid rules of normal life and all their efforts were directed at discovering a means of entering that other world. We should pause at this juncture: there was a way into the other world, but were there any clues or signposts to indicate the direction? Well, we are on the trail of an astonishing phenomenon: there were indeed clues and signposts. What is more, they were important, but we have to ask ourselves what their nature was and whether they still exist today. Can people in our time make use of them—you, for instance?"

The old man stopped in his tracks and looked straight at me.

"What a monumental task you are facing, to put into words the truth of what you saw when you decided to follow the horses. Had you not made a first, faltering step toward that other world? To convey to me what happened required practically no words. Because I had experienced the same thing I was able to read it in your eyes, but this other world I am telling you about is almost indescribably large. How is it possible for you, who are in this world, given that you intend to do so, to communicate what you know? You need to have another language; you need the language of pictures and symbols."

six

I COULDN'T HELP FIDDLING with the carved stone figures: I followed the curves of the nostrils with my finger, stuck my arm into their gaping mouths, caressed the curvaceous shapes of the marble statues, and ran my hand over the mosaic fragments. The mysterious figures in these spherical vaults seemed more powerful and inscrutable than any I had seen before. The flames of the candles gave off a reddish glow and produced a colorful effect of greater complexity than any light from a single source.

My afternoon's experiences still weighed heavily on me, but these figures had none of the supernatural atmosphere of those in the oval room. They were straightforward sculptures carved out of stone and wood or created from iron and glass. They were whimsical and bizarre: they ranged from lions, snakes, and eagles to centaurs, angels with countless eyes, and dragons with excised eyes and weird tails. I enjoyed running my hands over all these creatures and felt no hint of tiredness even though it was by now late in the evening.

I had ceased asking questions of the old man and simply followed his gentle guidance as I attempted to make sense of what I saw. Only by being alert could I show the deep respect I felt for him as he led me through the maze of rooms and introduced me to a world that was home and familiar territory to him. As my hand settled on a lion's bulging eyeball I asked myself, *Where will he take me today?*

He began speaking again.

"This world has its own laws. An ignorant person would make very little of it. The level at which these messages are transmitted is too complex. These sculptures are experiences from another dimension translated into objects. If you want to share this level of understanding, you have to open the portals of your soul. The senses live and work through artistic representations and you will have to learn to understand them. Centuries ago our whole world was characterized by these symbolic figures and it constituted an inexhaustible language.

"'*La lengua de los parajos*' is what the farmers in the valley call it. The understanding of this language of the soul has given way to a narrow, rational way of thought. The rich leaps of imagination, once hearts were stirred, and the wonderful harmony of body, soul, spirit, and nature are no longer with us. The door to that other world has been shut. If only we could penetrate that amazing world again, it would enable us to decipher the secret of your message."

During the night that followed, the old man taught me the first steps that would lead me into this mysterious other world. His words demystified even the most unprepossessing characters and sculptures; our understanding ranged in wonderful circles and conjured up a light, as bright as any fire, that lit up the darkness and showed us faces, countless faces, of what seemed to be a single reality.

There was only one being that drew no comment: the horse, in whatever form it appeared. A horse only had to make a brief appearance for his face to become motionless and for him to withdraw in silence. Although I was bubbling with a sense of enquiry, I dared not question him on the subject. However, I was given an enchanted vision of another world that seemed no longer to exist.

"Is it really gone forever, the 'other world'?" I asked him.

"No," he replied. "Your soul is intact. Humanity's spirit cannot be destroyed. It is alive and still strong. Souls live on and on as symbols."

seven

IN THE FIRST WEAK LIGHT of the new day, a small gaunt monk shut the heavy monastery doors behind us. With the help of two narrow bedrooms, we had the means of repairing the effects of a sleepless night. When we awoke, still dazed with our experience, I stood, enjoying the cool, damp morning air on my skin. We stood without speaking for a few moments and then I followed the old man across the inner court.

As we went to our left, a long narrow staircase led us up to a terrace with pale paving stones, surrounded by a stone balustrade. At the widest point, another smaller staircase led to an art gallery. I followed the old man in and we sat ourselves down on a bench. It was still dark outside: only the first feeble signs of the approaching day allowed us to pick out some distant features of the landscape around the monastery. I could only take a guess at how beautiful it might be.

The old man kept his eyes shut and for a long time I thought he might be sleeping. Then suddenly he said quietly, "It's the second day of the new moon. The day after tomorrow, the first little sickle of the new moon will lighten the sky a mere fraction. It was on a night such as this when, almost two thousand years ago, a number of holy men gathered to witness one of the most painful ceremonies imaginable. As usual, they were not sacrificing what to them was the holiest of holies, a magnificent white horse, but one of themselves."

Before our eyes where two hilltops stood guarding a flat valley between them, the day made its entrance. I was perched on the front of one stone bench, my hands in my lap to keep warm and my back hunched forward, whereas the old man sat proud and motionless, defying the cold, damp air. So I straightened up and lifted my head to await the new day and the conclusion of the monk's words.

"They sacrificed themselves?" I asked, in such a quiet voice that my words seemed not to have been intended for him but for myself, and for the shadows that stretched across the ground in front of us, and the sparkles made here and there by the sun catching the morning dew. Then the old man spoke.

"The Celtic priests practiced an unprecedented liberality, derived from an admirable freedom of thought. They were the guardians of tolerance: every single person could worship their own gods and nearly every family and every clan had their gods. They were not impractical people, and yet this dreadful event took place that night and, what is more, under the sign of the horse—indeed, the sign of the white horse. This event announced the painful retreat of the druids and the disappearance of the Celtic world, the world of our forebears."

Without giving a moment's thought to what I was about to say, I asked him, "Were they in love with life or death?"

The old man looked at me with a gentle smile on his exhausted features.

"They loved life because they had no fear of death. This is what they taught with enthusiasm, although they never called themselves teachers; teachers were all too often advocates of rigid rules instead of truths. They, on the other hand, were fully alive, and where there is life there cannot be rigid frameworks that have to be followed. Life begets liveliness and an ever stronger attraction to life itself. It is like an unbearable hunger, a longing that is only satisfied by the event, by life. Because they sought life so assiduously in everything, they only taught, 'Live! Live! For God's sake, live!'"

A thin veil of barely discernible light was touching the valley in front of us; the distant mountains were black silhouettes, sharply defined against the rosy dawn, until the stronger light swallowed the weaker and brought the sun.

Once again the old man returned to the subject I had already left behind and thereby concentrated on the fine details of the matter, the consideration of how the horse could be the medium through which man understands his existence. Why is the horse such a fundamental symbol? According to the old man, the secret of this symbol, the white horse of the Celts and on the Arms of the Templars, has been buried under a devious cloud of lies, fear, and ignorance.

This was apparently why he had been silent the previous night on the subject of any horses' images. He had no wish to engage with the wails of the despondent or the whimpering of the one-dimensional horse specialists. They were always asking themselves why the horse should have such a central role in the history of European culture — in pictures, myths, and sagas — but they never came up with an answer. The horse symbolized the sun and moon, they maintained. They discoursed on the mythical confrontation of the horse and the bullock and asked what was behind it. It was, they said, the battle of the sexes—that the horse symbolized the one that carried burdens, like water, and escorted the dead souls. They talked about the heroes who seized the gods' horses and took over their wonderful characteristics. Then there were the battles in which warrior and horse joined forces to fight evil, personified by fire-breathing dragons. But what did the dragons symbolize? Or the horse? And what was a hero? Why did so many heroes join battle with the help of a horse? Why indeed was it always a horse and not a camel or an elephant? Were there not other great animals that man has trained to accept riders? Why were so many of our myths and sagas peopled with men who were mounted on horses? Who could answer all these questions?

Consider the holy sacrifice of horses. In very different apparel, they once were part of the most important rituals. It was said that the holiest of all sacrifices was the horse, the white horse. But was it ever said why?

No! We needed another key, another clue to get at the secret. Why was it that in all these cases the horse was a part of the story? What was behind it? What happened on that moonless night, that awful event, was not an isolated case. It was a mystery not dissimilar to the case of the Celtic priests and druids, who vanished almost without trace, and also the Templars, that society of monks who valued the horse in the same way as did the druids.

The druids found themselves in opposition to the Romans, something the old man strangely failed to expand upon and in a way failed to explain at all. When the Templars, hundreds of years later, were persecuted by the Church and King Philip, although they were one of the most powerful groups in all Europe, they hardly resisted;

the Order of the Templars was destroyed and the fraternity dispersed over the whole of Europe, seeking refuge from Portugal to Scotland. Perhaps here was the thin thread that would lead us through the labyrinth? Was there a connection here? Who were these people and why did they disappear in this strange way?

A little story might explain this phenomenon, something that the most learned people today still find impossible to understand: Once upon a time a weird and wonderful animal with a brown coat joined battle with King Ailill's powerful white-horned bullock and he won, whereupon he gave three victory bellows. His fame spread throughout the land. What then was it that made him so famous? It was nothing more or less than the strength and ferocity of his adversary.

The Celtic priests, the Wise Men, the druids and the Templars all believed they were in possession of an ancient wisdom, that they were the guardians of the doors that led into the other world. At the same time, they lived fully in this world and with the knowledge of the world's laws of ebb and flow, of birth and death. The moon in its state of constant change has always made humanity aware that everything we can imagine is subject to these fundamental laws, including the rise and fall of entire cultures. Theirs was a dark age of destruction, conquest, rabble-rousing, and torture. Thus it was that the wise men vanished—because the times favored darkness. And they preferred to destroy themselves rather than fight against the inevitable and be annihilated. Had they done so, they knew they would only have strengthened the darkness—much as if they were to help the white-horned creature fight against the brown one.

However, this was not to be a setback forever. The seed remained, even if blown about by hurricanes, and one day sprouted fresh green shoots that would carry on the fight. This is a rule of the world: it is symbolized by the fight between the hero and the dragon, in whatever form it manifests itself. Dragons and monsters turn up in the real world in many different costumes. They are masters of disguise, like the wolf in sheep's clothing.

"The world," continued the old man after a moment's hesitation, "is not as it is because it has to be. It's the way it is because we have shaped it, but one man's work can be altered by another."

Thus we were on the trail of another truth that, like all truths, was hidden underneath a symbol. We were on the trail of the truth about horses. I had a question to ask, one so often asked by scholars: why was the symbol of the horse so widely used in all the mythical depictions of this cultural heritage? Was it perhaps because the horse symbol was able to embody the spirit of our forebears and their beliefs better than anything else in the visible world?

The old man paused for a long time before saying, "The things you sought and found among the horses were your first signposts to the other world: they manifest themselves in the symbols you find in pictures, but how will this world and the other hold together? The entrance from one to the other is through the eye of a needle—so small we can hardly imagine it, and how easily this connection between the world of man and the world of the gods is destroyed! When one of them is moving in heavenly ways, coming and going like the moon, and the other is not following, then what happens?"

"The worlds break apart. The connection is broken," I answered softly.

"And when man separates himself from the world of the gods, what is left?"

"The naked reality of what is visible," I said.

"Now, we have the key to hand: when the one world, in the process of changing, grows further apart from the creative force, then the umbilical cord is severed; humanity and matter ossify. Heaven and earth are pulled apart; violence and extermination rule on earth. The breath of the gods that warmed the soul of humanity is stilled and there is nothing but agitation.

"Life is movement; therefore, when the world grows stiff, death will be master. The other world is one of movement: the world of the gods is one of constant creation.

"The spirit is awake when it is growing, developing, stimulated, and active. Feelings are real when they vibrate in unison with the soul, when they stimulate themselves and others. The strength of a man is a judgment passed on both his physical and mental ability. Harmony is obtained when humanity strives for it without interruption, for harmony is not ossified—it is all to do with effort. Love is king in this world only when life is a combination of godliness, wisdom, strength, feeling, and peace, all working in unison. Love exists when everything is working and then God is working, too."

The old man looked at me, and the exhaustion had been washed from his placid features. He asked me, "Which being of all beings would you choose to symbolize this godly combination of strength, humility, purity, spirituality, and beauty, because it combines these qualities in the best possible way?"

"I would choose the horse," I replied.

eight

NOW, AT LAST THE OLD MAN rose to his feet and, as the sun stood above us at the highest point of its orbit, he said, "In your language the sun is feminine—you say '*die Sonne*,' because your language has deep roots. For our forefathers, the sun was feminine, as was the power of the gods. According to their tradition, men came from a distant land, created and born of women under the sign of the sun. Then the gods combined their three attributes into one being: the ability to give birth, far-sightedness, and the feminine virtue of unceasing creative toil with the light and power of the sun. The shape of this godly creation was none other than that of a white mare. She was Epona, the ancient goddess of the Celts.

"So it is that the white horse is the original early Christian symbol: According to them, Christ rode on a white horse and not on a donkey. It was the symbol of the seekers of the Holy Grail, of whom Parsifal was the 'Horse King.' The heroes achieved their success thanks to the strength of horses, because the horses were the symbol of the gods. By being able to harness the attributes of the gods they could defeat dragons who represented all that was wicked and dark, the inner self that had become atrophied by grasping after material gain. The horse is the symbol of the weight-bearer as well as of water, the original medium of the gods for bearing everything possible.

"If you want to get closer to horses for their benefit you must combine the three centers of your inner being into one:

"The power of all that is really alive;

"Love that is the queen of all emotions;

"The knowledge that is the fruit of your mind.

"Then shout to the rocks:

"*It is not any old horse!*

"*It is not any old white horse!*

"It is the incarnation of the oldest gods, the symbol of a free, animated, evolving, and ever-self-renewing being. This signal comes like a shooting star into the world to announce a new beginning, a revolution.

"It is a symbol of the female against unjust and brutal subjugation.

"It is a symbol of the resistance, over thousands of years, against the willful damage to our culture."

He stared into my face as he continued, "Only by a supreme effort can you achieve the deed, and only the deed can lead to freedom! Follow the symbol of the white horse, because it is the symbol of our true inner selves, and for two thousand years it has been the symbol of liberation."

nine

AS THE SUN BEGAN TO SET, we reached the old monk's house. I looked down into the valley and listened to the sound of Vali in his paddock, slowly chewing his alfalfa. Every time I looked in that direction the landscape appeared as a different set of colors and shapes, and sometimes left me with the impression that I was looking at this view for the first time.

The sun was concealed by a low layer of clouds, and the depths of the lake seemed almost to vibrate with a mysterious shade of blue.

The rocks that lay around the margins of the lake pierced the silvery mist, and where they were at their highest, the sun, playing across the tops of the clouds, caught them in a noose of copper light that stood out against the blue water and the white clouds.

Their inner spirit left few traces, I thought to myself, which explains why they remain so hidden from us. They built no monuments but concentrated on building their inner selves so there is hardly a single material witness to their existence. All that remains is their modesty, a mere shadow of their lives on this earth, and the virgin soil to nurture those to be born.

It was on this evening that an understanding grew into a certainty: the understanding that this symbol of the horse is a living symbol of a world that appears to have disappeared but in which everything still exists.

I felt a comforting flow that seemed to spring from my throat and spread throughout my body. Here was something I could trust completely, that embraced and consumed every anxious thought. It was of a warm and beautiful nature that came from within the physical shell of my body, and, after filling every cranny, emerged on the outside to combine with all that was similar.

We spent the days that followed together with our horses and from time to time the old man extended a hardly perceptible invitation to me to watch him at work. I spent many hours each day with Vali and recognized how much I had yet to learn and to experience. For the first time I was a real pupil: a pupil of the old man, a pupil of the horse, and a pupil of life.

It was now that I became aware of the weakness that had been a part of the old Vali. It worried me to see how he began to perspire when the day was still young and the air fresh. It worried me no end to notice how sometimes he seemed almost to stop breathing for a moment; I noticed how his flanks heaved and then stopped as suddenly as they had begun, how the tiredness in his eyes appeared all the more often to cloak his inner fire, how his footsteps were growing unsteady and his lips dry and chapped.

I asked the old man for his advice, thinking that possibly the reason still lay in the way I treated Vali.

"No," he replied, "it's not your fault. It's time passing—it's the years, the coming and the going."

And then one morning as I approached the old shepherd house where Vali lived, there was no head looking out to greet me on my arrival. I already knew the reason. My footsteps slowed and I felt the blood draining from my face. Slowly I opened the gate, and there he lay. I leaned down and stroked his neck: it was still warm.

What a life and what suffering! And what a good teacher you were to me! It all makes sense, I thought. *You have not struggled in vain. I will give something in return, either to humanity or to horses.*

For a long time I left my hand lying on his neck, until at last the tears began to flow. I was filled with sadness and thankfulness in equal measure.

The midday sun rose high enough to shine over the stable door and add a dull luster to the dead horse's hide.

"Yes, Vali, there was a reason for it all," I told him.

I thought of all the injustice he had suffered not only from others but from me, because of my fury and hate for him who wanted so badly to live and be understood.

Down in the valley where the soil was soft, we dug a deep trench and then carefully dragged his corpse down the stony side of the hill and buried him.

I spent many days sitting in this spot, thinking of all that I had been through, of how it all began, of Vali and the old monk, and little by little I came to terms with it all.

I thought of Paloma and the village where she lived, of the lake and the wild horses.

I beat a simple rhythm in the sand with my feet and sang a dirge as many peoples all around the world do. The simple melody repeated itself and gradually helped me to marry the little mound in front of me with the beauty of the mountains around me.

I had all the time in the world: There was nothing there and yet there was everything there. Vali's death made it clear to me that it was time to say goodbye and move on. Nothing has ever quite seemed the same to me since that day and there is no need to speak about it anymore.

Like a fledgling bird that makes a few trial flights before flying away from the nest, so my time with the old man drew to a close. Little by little I began to distance myself from him, from our house, and from the mountains. All the paths I knew so well, I traversed once again. I was thankful for all that I had been through. It was time to close the book, only to find that a new one opened, a new beginning.

The day arrived when I said good-bye to the old man. He asked for nothing. He said nothing. I gathered up my few belongings and set off down the path to the village—passing the little mound in the valley.

ten

I HAVE NOT SEEN THE MONK again to this day, nor have I heard from him. We never wrote to each other.

Of all I learned during that period, I have only been able to put into practice a very small part of it in the world of humans and horses, but whenever it comes to writing something, I think to myself how right the old man was.

So it is that today I am embarked on a search for myself, for the origins of my world, for the truth, for the truth of that being who will never let me go. Sometimes, when I have the feeling that I have found a being who will make me as happy as I can possibly be, then all my energy is directed into listening, into taking and seeking advice, warmth, and comfort: in the message from the horse, the message from the silent ones.

The old keep their counsel for long
periods—so long that no one listens any more.
One that seeks the truth—and there are
quite a number of them that know
the truth—why are they silent?

—The Old Monk